Nina Milne has always dreamed of writing for Mills & Boon—ever since she played libraries with her mother's stacks of Mills & Boon romances as a child. On her way to this dream Nina acquired an English degree, a hero of her own, three gorgeous children and—somehow!—an accountancy qualification. She lives in Brighton and has filled her house with stacks of books—her very own *real* library.

THEIR CHRISTMAS ROYAL WEDDING

NINA MILNE

MILLS & BOON

This is a work of fiction. Names, characters, places, locations
and incidents are purely fictional and bear no relationship to
any real life individuals, living or dead, or to any actual places,
business establishments, locations, events or incidents.
Any resemblance is entirely coincidental.

Published in Great Britain 2019
by Mills & Boon, an imprint of HarperCollins*Publishers*
1 London Bridge Street, London, SE1 9GF

© 2019 Harlequin Books S.A.

Special thanks and acknowledgement are given to Nina Milne
for her contribution to the A Crown by Christmas series

ISBN: 978-0-263-08126-8

MIX
Paper from
responsible sources
FSC® C007454

Printed and bound in Great Britain
by CPI Group (UK) Ltd, Croydon, CR0 4YY

To the lovely community of romance writers
for being so kind and helpful!

CHAPTER ONE

Royal Palace, Aguilarez, November

HIS ROYAL HIGHNESS Prince Cesar of Aguilarez looked down from the helicopter at the looming trees, the jut and crags of the mountainous terrain as the pilot began their descent to the helipad that topped the fortress-like palace he had grown up in. A palace he had visited only infrequently in the past three years. When need dictated.

The whir of the blades couldn't distract him from the grim tone of his thoughts. Now he'd been summoned back to a family summit—called, presumably, to figure out a strategy in the face of the scandal that had rocked the royal House of Asturias. And not just the house, but also the royal family of Valenti, rulers of the neighbouring country of Casavalle.

Two small countries that shared the same island—shared also a history of feuding and war. A relentless succession of invasion attempts had left both countries battle-scarred, until eventually a fragile peace had been negotiated. A peace that had endured for over two centuries as both countries had prospered.

A peace now under threat.

All because of his younger sister Meribel.

What had she been thinking? Like all five royal siblings Meribel had been brought up to know that Aguilarez came first, that duty was paramount, and emotions were an irrelevance.

So Meribel's actions defied belief. To date she'd jilted Crown Prince Luca Valenti days before their wedding. Whilst pregnant with another man's baby. The whole idea of the marriage had been to cement an alliance; now the alliance was in tatters.

Then they'd been hit by the next scandal, because it turned out that the Crown Prince of Casavalle wasn't the Crown Prince after all, because Luca had a long-lost, hitherto unknown older sister—Gabriella Ross.

To compound the situation Gabriella's existence had been discovered six months after the death of Casavalle's King, so just before Luca was due to ascend the throne of Casavalle. Now Gabriella Ross, a woman brought up in Canada, with no knowledge of her heritage or the royal blood that coursed through her veins, would take the throne.

The whole situation was a mess and little wonder the people of both Casavalle and Aguilarez were crying foul, with accusations of deceit and counter deceit on all sides.

Hence the summons to Cesar, requesting his presence at the Aguilarean palace. Though the request had been an order and, whilst he understood the need for a meeting, the manner of the summons tasted bitter in his throat: a curt demand with no hint of family affection. No surprise really—the Asturias family didn't do affection. Thus it had always been and thus it always would be.

No matter, he was here now, and as he alighted onto the helipad he braced himself as if for an ordeal, even as he inhaled the fresh snow-tanged mountain air with a sense of appreciation that he had come home to the country he loved.

Minutes later he entered the throne room, where his parents were already seated at the enormous circular wooden table, faces serious. Behind them up on a dais, the imposing stone throne embedded with jewels, the spoils of victories of the distant past, dominated the room. The surrounding walls were adorned with tapestries and paintings that depicted past battles and a pair of crossed swords topped the marble fireplace.

'You've cut it fine, Cesar,' King Jorge said. 'We are due in Casavalle for talks in a few hours and we have much to discuss.'

As he bowed first to his father and then his mother Cesar switched to ambassador mode, the role he'd been brought up to, destined for from the day of his birth. 'Apologies, Father.'

Present no reason as it will only be seen as an excuse.

His mother now. 'First we must talk about Lady Amelia.'

'We must?' Cesar could not imagine why this would be necessary—Lady Amelia Scott-Browne was his current girlfriend, though he was pretty sure a break-up was imminent. There had been signs of possessiveness, signs that Lady Amelia had forgotten the rules she'd signed up to. First and foremost being no long-term future. Because Cesar had no intention of getting married. Marriage equalled a bullet he fully intended to dodge. After all, he was the spare heir—there was no necessity for him to marry. Both his brothers had been marched to the altar, both had produced the requisite heirs. So there was no need for him to be entrapped in an unwanted union.

'Yes, Cesar, we must. You need to end the…association.' His mother made a small moue of distaste.

'Why?' It seemed a fair question; his parents had never interfered in his 'associations' before. Rather they tended to simply pretend they did not exist.

The King leant forward. 'Because we have a plan.'

'What plan?' Foreboding prickled his neck as he faced his parents.

'The best way to forge an alliance and show the world that Aguilarez and Casavalle are still friends is through marriage. So, Cesar. You will marry the new Crown Princess of Casavalle. Gabriella Ross will become your bride.'

Cesar felt the loom of the metaphorical wall at his back, could hear the hiss of the oncoming bullet.

Royal Palace of Casavalle, December

It was no good. Sleep was not going to happen. Gabi had counted two thousand seven hundred and five sheep, tried deep breathing, reminded herself that it was practically sinful not to be able to sleep on sheets this luxurious, surrounded by every comfort a queen-in-waiting could expect. But all to no avail; her brain buzzed and whirled with too many thoughts to allow sleep.

Queen-in-waiting. The words caromed around her brain, underlay every waking thought, every dream-filled night, and the bizarre surrealism made the whole situation seem nigh on impossible. How could she, Gabriella Ross, be royalty? For thirty-one and a half years of her life she had believed herself to be an ordinary person; she'd been brought up by her ordinary, elderly aunt and uncle in a small town in the Canadian mountains. She had inherited their bookshop, which she had adored, had built it into a thriving business—that had been her life.

Now…here she was in the palace of Casavalle. All because eight months ago she'd found two letters, written by her mother, who'd died when she was only three. One letter to King Vincenzo of Casavalle and one letter written to Gabriella herself.

Letters that revealed Gabi's true identity, the fact that her father had been King Vincenzo Valenti. A father she would never know, who had never known of her existence. The irony was obvious: in all her childhood reckonings, when she'd spent so many hours wondering who her father was, one of her fantasies had been that she was a secret princess. A fantasy she'd long since outgrown.

Giving up on the attempt to sleep, she sat up, propped up by sumptuous pillows on a mattress neither too hard nor too soft. As she looked round the shadowy splendour of the room, furnished in gold and red, a verdant Christmas tree in the corner, redolent with twinkling lights and beautiful painted baubles, a sudden burst of homesickness nipped her. Her tiny bedroom in Crystal Lake, the simple pine furniture, a poster of a hockey-player crush from her teen years still tacked up in her wardrobe…

Stop.

There was so much to be thankful for: she'd gone from having no family at all after the death of her aunt and uncle to gaining two brothers, both of whom she had bonded with instantly. As an added bonus Luca, a true prince, had fallen for Gabi's best friend, Imogen. And Antonio, her next brother, was soon to be married to Tia, who Gabi already loved. In addition, Queen Maria, the princes' mother, had welcomed her with dignity, grace and warmth. They all had.

Yet…guilt still haunted Gabi. Luca had been brought up believing himself to be the heir to Casavalle and now he had to stand aside for her. The impact on the whole family she had wanted so badly and already loved brought her disquiet. Along with an overwhelming fear that she couldn't do it; couldn't be the fair, just, wise ruler Casavalle deserved.

She didn't even know how to look the part. That was why sleep eluded her, held ransom by her nerves—because in mere hours that evening it was her Presentation Ball and the very idea caused her insides to curl in sheer horror. Because it was imperative she pull this off.

For the good of both Casavalle and Aguilarez, she had to win people over to her cause, try to stem the after-effects of the scandals that rippled the country and caused unrest. But that meant she had to face all the dignitaries, her every movement scrutinised both at home and abroad. Had to face the Royal family of Asturias, including the formidable Prince Cesar, who, rumour had it, was less than pleased at being recalled home from his ambassadorial duties.

Sometimes it felt that simply by existing she was causing so very many problems. Life for both royal houses would have been easier if she hadn't found out the truth. The feeling horribly familiar—as a child she had known her aunt's and uncle's lives would have been easier, happier without having been burdened with Gabi. Peter and Bea had been an elderly childless couple, who had been unexpectedly landed with Gabi. And now Gabi had landed in Maria's… Luca's… Antonio's lives, had upended their lives just as much as she had Peter's and Bea's.

It was no use; she couldn't lie in all this splendour any more—the doubts, the weight of responsibility, the fear of making a fool of herself would crush her into the soft pillows and suffocate her.

She swung her legs over the sumptuous mattress and wriggled her toes into the soft plushness of the carpet. Pulled on jeans and an oversized sweater over her flannel pyjamas, tugged on a pair of running shoes. Maybe she'd tiptoe into the kitchens and make herself some camomile tea or even get a snack—she'd eaten nothing at dinner, too nervous at the idea of the ball.

Carefully she snuck down the vast passageway, told herself that there was no need to sneak—technically this was her palace. Only it didn't work like that—here she was hemmed in by rules and shibboleths, a hem woven by fear of bringing the Valenti name into further disrepute. As her mother had over thirty years before. Sophia Valenti had fled her royal marriage without explanation, deserted her husband and vanished in the dead of night. Once the scandal had died down she'd been written out of Casavallian history as the shortest of footnotes.

As she approached the kitchens Gabi's courage failed her. Despite the lateness of the hour she could hear activity, staff preparing for the next days and weeks. For the ball, for Christmas—it seemed as if the palace never slept. The idea of appearing unannounced seemed impossible; after all, she didn't even know where the teabags were...or if packets of cookies even existed in the royal lexicon.

It was then the idea came to her: she knew exactly where she wanted to be. The stables. There she knew she would find some calm and peace, with the magnificent beings that didn't care whether she was a princess or not. There would be no judgement. Plus, just that day a gift of two beautiful horses had arrived from Aguilarez—

and, ridiculous though it might sound, Gabi was worried they were homesick. She'd only been able to spend a few snatched minutes with them, posed for a photo and now suddenly it felt imperative to go check on them.

Before she could change her mind she tiptoed past the kitchens, along the vast corridor to a side door that led to the paved courtyard. Opening it quietly, she slipped out, braced herself against the cold bite of the winter wind, inhaled the tang of promised snow in the air. A scent so familiar and yet so different from the Canadian equivalent. She crossed the mosaic tiles, suddenly aware of the dead quiet of the night.

She entered the stables and instantly a sense of peace, of comfort, enveloped her and she headed straight for the stalls that housed the new arrivals. Gently she stroked the nose of the nearest, heard his whinny and moved closer to his warmth. If only these creatures could attend the ball tomorrow instead of the Asturias royal family.

A noise interrupted her fanciful thoughts, the sound of footsteps, the rustle of a coat… All sense of tranquillity disappeared, replaced by instant panic. Fear that she would be caught, a suspicion that royalty did not roam the stables in the wee hours of the morning with jeans pulled over their pyjamas. Instinct propelled her into the next-door stall and she dived down into the straw, lay still, her heart pounding her ribcage.

Cesar Asturias muttered under his breath as he crossed the courtyard of the Casavalle palace, having exited the palace after yet another meeting between the Asturiases and the Valentis. The whole situation had gone from bad to worse; the position seemed inescapable. He'd been called on to make the ultimate sacrifice: a political marriage. The diplomat in him applauded and accepted the necessity, saw that it would cement the alliance between Casavalle and Aguilarez, show the world that the Asturiases and the Valentis accepted Gabriella Ross as rightful Queen. The marriage would cancel out the insult of Meribel's defection. The irony was not lost on him. Meribel had baulked at the last hurdle, decided she couldn't go through with a loveless marriage for the sake of duty. So now it was Cesar's turn to step up. So here he was, ready to attend Gabriella Ross's Presentation Ball the following day.

The start of Campaign Marriage.

Because it was a campaign and he would plan it as carefully as any general had ever planned a military campaign. Obviously nowadays a royal bride and groom could not be forced into a marriage. And, as his father had pointed out, Gabriella Ross had not been brought up as royalty, might not understand or accept the convention of a marriage of political convenience. 'So you will have to approach this carefully, Cesar. Make the girl fall in love with you,' King Jorge had ordered.

'No.' Cesar's reaction had been unequivocal. 'I will not do that, Father, but I will convince Gabriella to marry me. But I ask you all—' he'd looked around the room, at his parents and Queen Maria '—to leave it to me. I do not want Gabriella to be instructed or coerced or "persuaded" by any of you. We have all seen how wrong that went with Meribel. I will do things my way.'

So it had been agreed that Queen Maria would not mention the proposed union to her sons or Gabriella. And thus began his first steps towards a ball and chain, the imprisonment of marriage.

Dark thoughts swirled as he headed towards his car,

and then he heard a whinny from the stables nearby. Another spurt of irritation huffed through him; he'd been horrified to learn that in a further 'gesture of goodwill' his family had gifted Gabriella two thoroughbred horses, one of whom Cesar himself was particularly fond.

His objections had been overruled.

No surprise there, then.

He remembered his father's cold, emotionless voice.

'The gift was necessary. If all goes well you will own those horses with Gabriella anyway.'

His mother, faintly exasperated.

'You are irrational, Cesar. You have hardly even been to Aguilarez these past years. To claim affection for these horses is nonsensical.'

There you had it: in the Asturias clan if something made no sense it was invalid. Emotions made no sense, hence his parents' marriage: a cold union, that had nonetheless produced five children. They had been faithful to each other yet not once had he ever seen either offer the other a sign of intimacy or simple affection. No wonder Cesar had vowed from an early age that marriage wasn't for him, had revelled in his bachelor lifestyle. Made sure he had enjoyed life, ensured every relationship included fun and passion in the short term. Now a similar fate to his parents' was before him; worst of all he understood that it was necessary.

A noise intruded on his thoughts, the soft whicker of a horse. Hell—it must be a sign. Perhaps he'd go and say hello to Ferron—nonsensical or not, he was fond of the beast. But as he entered the stables he halted, suddenly sure he wasn't alone. There had been movement, an indrawn breath, a rustle of fabric. Swiftly he moved forward towards Ferron's stall, saw the beautiful horse was fine. Noiselessly he moved towards the next-door stall, pushed the door open and stepped inside, all his senses on alert. Could be a saboteur, a horse thief...?

Surely that was a figure lying in the straw. Hoping to evade detection? Swiftly he pulled his phone from his pocket, turned on the torch, held the light up and blinked; there on the straw lay one of the most beautiful women he'd seen in his life. Long chestnut hair, straight classical nose, high cheekbones. And impossible, nay, criminal, to ignore the length of her slim curvy figure, clad in jeans and oversized jumper, over...he squinted at the cuffs of her wrist...checked flannel pyjamas.

OK, Cesar. Time to stop staring and time instead to figure out why Gabriella Ross, Crown Princess of Casavalle and his possible bride-to-be, was hiding in a bed of straw.

CHAPTER TWO

GABI LIFTED A hand to shield herself from the intrusive beam of light and instantly the man holding the torch redirected the rays to the floor. What to do, what to do? What on earth had possessed her to hide? Stupid, stupid, stupid. The urge to weep from sheer mortification was tempting but she refused to succumb.

Instead she had to embark on mission impossible to try and salvage even a semblance of dignity. As she looked up at the man, he stooped and held out a hand. 'May I help you up, Your Royal Highness?'

Fabulous; he'd recognised her. Any forlorn hope that she could somehow pretend to be a fainting groom faded.

'Thank you,' she murmured, figuring a hand up would be more dignified than a clumsy scramble to her feet.

His hand encircled hers, his grip cool and firm as he helped her up and then stood back. She darted a look at him, his face cast in shadows, the torch now by his side so she couldn't see him clearly. Yet even in the gloom she registered handsome features and the bemusement that etched them. Dark short hair, strong features, firm jaw, tall, muscled body dressed in clothes that discreetly indicated expense. His dark grey woollen coat moulded broad shoulders and to her irritation she felt a sudden surge of…interest.

Get a grip.

This man was a stranger in the Casavalle stables; belatedly she wondered if she should be scared. Yet he looked vaguely familiar. Oh, God. Was he perhaps someone she should know? She had been introduced to so many people over the past weeks it was nearly impossible to remember them all, though she was trying.

But surely she would remember who he was…if she'd met him before… She couldn't imagine forgetting a man with such a potent aura.

An aura that was messing with her head, making it whirl and think with her hormones rather than her common sense. Not the behaviour of a queen in waiting; she'd learnt that much. *Think, Gabi.* He was in the stables at midnight—good chance, then, that he had a reason to be here; something to do with the horses. Perhaps he'd been sent with the gift from the Asturias family, with Ferron and Arya. That would make sense. Perhaps she'd spotted him earlier in that whirlwind press photo and registered his presence. Maybe he'd come in to check on them.

Doubt flickered in her mind—to be brutally honest he didn't look like a groom, but she still didn't understand the hierarchy of how the royal entourage worked. Not that it mattered. The man was connected to the horses in some capacity—she didn't need to know any more than that. Right now what mattered was that she should stop gawping at him. Royalty did not gawp.

'Thank you,' she said. 'And…um…sorry about that.' She gestured to the straw with what she could only hope was a poised rueful smile. Knew it was more likely to be a grimace. 'I was checking the horses. Sounds stupid but I was worried they may be a little homesick.'

An arrested look came to his face, and his dark brown eyes flashed with empathy, surely a confirmation that this man must be connected somehow with the horses.

He smiled at her. 'That makes sense, or, if it does not, I do understand and appreciate it. But why the straw?' Reaching out, he pulled a bit out of her hair.

Gabi was pretty sure there was some royal protocol or other that made the gesture punishable by death. Yet this man made the move seem natural.

'I...you startled me and I just...dived for cover. I hadn't realised someone else would be coming to check the horses. I'm so sorry to interrupt your work here. Please proceed with your duties.'

For a fleeting second an expression she couldn't interpret crossed his face, and then he took the smallest of steps backwards, executed a bow.

'Ma'am. There is no need for you to apologise. These horses are now yours and are yours to visit any time of day and night. I know they will appreciate your care.'

'And I'm sure that they appreciated yours. Tell me, are you their...?' She allowed her voice to question and he took another small step backwards.

'I have been responsible for them. I stopped by to-night to ensure they have settled in, that they are not, as you say, "homesick". Soon I will return to Aguilarez.' He hesitated, studied her face. 'If you like, before I go, we could take a moonlit ride; you could get to know Ferron and Arya better.'

Her turn to hesitate now; were royal princesses supposed to go on moonlit rides with strangers? Possibly not...*but*...her brain scrambled into overdrive, wanting, seeking reasons to justify her instinctive desire to say yes. This man wasn't a stranger as such—he was part of the Aguilarez entourage. So this could be classed as a gesture of friendliness. Also he must love these horses and probably wanted a chance to have one last ride— it would be unkind to deny him that. And royalty often rode out accompanied by staff, and maybe she could use this as a fact-finding mission. Find out more about the Asturias family before the ball, especially Prince Cesar. And…dammit…she wanted to do this. Craved a ride on one of these magnificent animals in the company of this man.

'Thank you. I'd like that. As long as you don't have to be back…'

'No. I do not need to leave yet.' He gestured outside. 'It is beautiful outside but cold—if it is not too presumptuous, I could lend you my coat.'

'But then you'll be cold.'

'I am used to these temperatures, ma'am; I grew up here. My jumper will suffice.' With a smile that rocked her backwards he hitched off his coat and handed it to her.

'Thank you, though I suspect I'll look ridiculous.' Though perhaps no more ridiculous than she already did, with bits of her pyjamas protruding at wrist and ankle.

'I'll saddle them up,' he said.

'We'll saddle them up,' she corrected. 'Which one would you prefer to ride? Ferron?' After all, he'd gone to Ferron's stall first—perhaps that was his preferred mount.

'I would like that,' he said.

Gabi couldn't help but observe as he saddled the horse; his actions were deft and fluid as he tucked the stirrups under the saddle, manoeuvred the buckles of the girth—whatever his role he was familiar and comfortable around horses and Ferron seemed more than content. His murmured words and gentle touch demonstrated clearly that he was known to this horse and any minor doubts faded away.

Soon they had led the horses out and mounted.

'Where to?' he asked.

'Through the woodlands,' she suggested.

'Sure.' As he patted Ferron's neck and they set off curiosity beset her. Now out in the moonlight she could see him more clearly, saw that his hands were smooth, his clothes definitely expensive.

'So, have you worked for the royal family for long?'

'All my life. You could say it is a family tradition.' His voice was tinged with a low irony.

'Do you regret it?' she asked, and he frowned as if he wished he'd not given so much away.

'Not at all, but it is sometimes hard to have your life preordained.'

'I liked that about mine. My old life, I mean.'

'You worked in a book store in Canada.'

'I did more than that. My uncle and aunt owned the store and I inherited it on their death.' Peter and Bea had passed away within months of each other and Gabi had grieved them deeply. She had loved them and would always be grateful to them for taking her in, for sacrificing their own dream for her. Without them, the knowledge she was alone in the world had been difficult.

But after a while her natural drive had come into force and she had thrown herself into her work. Kept up with her teaching schedule, where she taught children and adults with reading difficulties, whilst working all other hours to make a success of the bookshop. 'It may seem like peanuts compared to ruling a kingdom but I loved my shop and it was thriving.' She could only hope it still was—she'd hired a manager to run it, still called as often as she could.

'And you had no idea of your heritage.'

'None.' She tried to keep bleakness from her tone, knew she hadn't when he guided Ferron closer to her, as if his presence could offer comfort.

'Then this must be hard,' he stated.

Gabi turned to him, met the directness of his gaze. 'You are one of the few people to have said that.' And he was. Many believed that she should be thrilled at her 'elevation' to a position of fame, fortune and power.

'Most people have a distorted view of royalty, that it is all about glamour and money and fame. That is part of it but there is a flip side to that coin.'

'Yes...the rules, the...' Gabi trailed off, suddenly aware that she mustn't sound as if she were complaining; that would not be within the Princesses' Behavioural Code either. 'Differences are hard sometimes. It is an enormous adjustment.' Change had come, huge, sweeping, terrifying change. Leaning down, she patted the horse's neck, knew she needed to direct the questions away from her. Because for some reason this man was disconcertingly easy to talk to.

'But what about you? You said you work for the royal family due to family tradition. Surely you're not bound to them.'

For a moment discomfort touched his aquiline features, dappled and shadowed in the moonlight that filtered the leafy glade. 'Tradition is important. My job pleases me…my life is a good one. I did not mean to sound as though I have regrets.'

Yet somehow she was sure he did and Gabi frowned, suddenly concerned. 'You know that I won't tell anyone about this conversation, or say that you have reservations about your work.'

Now he smiled, the smile warm and full of reassurance and it caused her tummy to flip as he reached out to touch her reins, careful, though, not to touch her and stupid regret coursed through her. 'I thank you, ma'am, and I assure you too that this conversation is confidential. But I do not fear the Asturias family.'

'Lucky you! I do…' The words fell from her lips without her intent, meant to be light but she suspected they had wobbled with fear.

'Why?' Curiosity and a sharpness touched his voice. 'What have they done?'

'No…they've done nothing. It's me. I am…worried. It's my presentation ball tomorrow…well, later today, this evening and, to be honest, I'm terrified.'

'Of the Asturias royals?'

'Not only of them. Of everything. If I'd been born to this, I would know what I'm doing. But I wasn't and I don't. There are so many things that could go wrong. I could say the wrong thing to the wrong person and spark a political row. I could fall on my bu— fall over, or use the wrong fork, or get spinach stuck between my teeth. I'll be on display to everyone and I'm dreading it.'

'You have nought to dread. You are royal and, if I may say, you are beautiful—you will dazzle the guests.'

Her skin heated at the man's words, because as he said them his gaze lingered on her and she felt a sudden shiver run through her. Of course, she knew he was just trying to make her feel better—she wasn't beautiful. Her hair was her best feature, long, glossy and chestnut, but she had no idea what to do with it. As for the rest of her, she was ordinary, veering at gawky at five feet eight.

'That's kind, but I don't want to dazzle anyone. All I want is to get through without making a fool of myself. I want people to believe I can do this role, can be a queen. And I doubt I'll be able to convince the Asturiases of that, especially Prince Cesar.'

Her companion stilled. 'Why do you say that?'

Gabi sighed, unsure why she was confiding in this man. Perhaps because she hoped, as a long-term staff member, he would reassure her. According to all she had learnt Prince Cesar had hardly been back home for years, his life a glittering ambassadorial whirl of diplomacy, travel and parties, usually with a beautiful woman on his arm. 'Apparently Prince Cesar is angered at being recalled home to attend this ball and be presented to me.'

The man hesitated. 'I would not trust gossip, ma'am. Prince Cesar is an ambassador. He will not be angered by the need to attend a ball for political reasons—that is his job.'

Gabi shook her head, suddenly realising she was gossiping. 'Perhaps he simply doesn't want to dance with me,' she said lightly. 'I have to dance the opening dance with him and he's probably heard I can't dance for toffee.' Another reason to panic.

'I am sure you underestimate yourself. I can see your natural grace from the way you ride.'

'That's different.' Yet the compliment warmed her. 'I've ridden since I was a teenager.' A hobby and a love that had also got her out from under her aunt and uncle's feet; aware that she had intruded into their life, Gabi had always done her best to give them space, wherever she could. 'Until I came to Casavalle I never danced, especially not a waltz. Now I have to waltz with a stranger with everyone watching me.' The idea made her shiver even in the warmth of his coat. Even worse that it was a stranger who was reputed to dislike her, whatever her companion said. 'And, believe me, I am the despair of my dance teacher.'

'I believe you will be fine, ma'am. You must have faith in yourself; imagine yourself as you are now. I promise you, if you have the grace and ability to ride a horse such as Arya you *can* waltz.'

His voice was full of conviction and she turned to him, felt her heart hop skip and jump at the strength of his words, wished she could siphon off some of that belief. 'It is not only about the waltz,' she admitted softly. 'It's the bigger picture too; I hope I'll be able to do my job and act the part of Crown Princess.'

'This is not a role, ma'am. You have no need to act a part; you are the Crown Princess, soon to be Queen.' His voice, low and vibrant, seemed to ripple off the evergreen branches of the trees and into the silvery moonlit air. 'This is not a part that can be abandoned at will, it is what you were born to be, albeit unwittingly.'

For a moment panic descended in a weighty thud and she could almost imagine her shoulders bowed. But she wouldn't let it show. As if in sympathy the moon scudded behind the clouds and she became aware of the time. 'We should turn back.'

'Ma'am?'

'Yes.'

He opened his mouth as if to speak and then gave a

small shake of his head. 'No matter. You're right. We should get back.'

They rode back in a silence broken only by the soft thud of the horses' hooves on the turf. But she couldn't help but study her companion, marvel at the tug of attraction she felt. He was not her type of man at all. The few men she'd dated in the past had all been average, pleasant…safe. This man was none of those. Though he'd been courteous, she sensed he would wield ruthlessness wherever necessary. As for safe—she could still feel the touch of his fingers in her hair as he'd brushed away the straw. Perhaps it was for the best that tonight he would return to his royal duties in Aguilarez; if she saw him again it would be a flash of a familiar face in a retinue.

They arrived at the stables; he dismounted with a lithe grace and headed towards her to help her alight. Hurriedly Gabi removed her foot from the stirrup and swung her leg over the horse's back. Too hurriedly as it turned out. The horse shook her head and pranced. Caught in the length of the borrowed coat, Gabi lost her usual balance and with a muttered curse slid in an ungainly fashion from the horse.

Was caught in a firm hold that steadied her whilst also sending her pulse rate into overdrive. She could smell his aftershave and the woodsy smell made her dizzy. She could feel the hard muscle of his body against her back, his arms around her waist.

For a heartbeat they remained standing there and then he released her, stepped back and she turned. Their eyes caught and he cleared his throat; dark brown eyes seemed to sear into her own. 'I should have remembered…to warn you… Arya always gets a bit spooked when you dismount.'

'It's OK. I should've known to take more care with a horse that doesn't know me.' Her voice too breathless as awareness swirled around them. He was so close she could reach out and touch him, so close that if she took a step forward and stood on tiptoe she could kiss him...

As if his mind travelled the same path his eyes darkened and desire sparked and ignited. 'Your coat,' she managed, through lips that seemed parched. Quickly she shrugged out of it, handed it over.

'Thank you.' Another stretch of silence and then, 'You had better get back in. I will tend to the horses.'

'Thank you for the escort and the midnight ride.' She wanted to say more, knew she couldn't. After all, she could hardly ask for a repeat date.

'You're very welcome, ma'am. And, truly, you have no need to worry about the ball tomorrow. You will dazzle everyone, including Prince Cesar. I know it.'

'Th...thank you.' Her brain seemed to be on auto repeat, because in truth their bodies were talking a whole different language. As if propelled by her hormones alone Gabi stepped forward, saw the man's eyes glance to her lips then back up to her face. For a second she thought he was going to kiss her, felt her lips part and her eyes close in sheer toe-tingling anticipation. Tried to grab onto common sense—princesses did not kiss strangers in the palace stables.

As if he recalled the same, he held out his hand, took hers and, lifting it to his lips, he kissed it. The old-fashioned gesture sent a shiver down her spine, and she wanted, yearned to take the initiative, step forward and cup his face, brush her lips against his.

But she couldn't. She mustn't. Because she was the

Crown Princess on the morning of her presentation ball.
So she did nothing.

'Goodbye, ma'am.'

'Goodbye…' As he headed to the stables she watched
him walk away, realised she didn't even know his name,
wondered if she would ever see her mystery man again.
Not, of course, that he was hers… That would be ridiculous.

CHAPTER THREE

CESAR ENTERED THE glittering ballroom, which was resplendent with Christmas glory. Two enormous, magnificently decorated trees shone and twinkled and filled the air with the scent of pine and festivity. Lit chandeliers hung in illuminated splendour from the vaulted ceilings. Wreaths adorned the walls, and the arches and pillars were festooned with trails of greenery. Cesar walked behind his parents, flanked by his older brothers and their wives and his younger sister Flavia. The united front of the Asturias family had scrubbed up well: his mother's ash-blonde hair sported the famous Asturian diamond tiara, her ice-blue gown was elegant and an echo of her eyes; his father and brothers looked supremely regal in their tuxes, their wives suitably designer-gowned and all gracious smiles. Flavia nudged him in the ribs. 'I feel sorry for poor Princess Gabriella. We look like an invading force for all our smiles.'

Now guilt pulsed as he remembered Gabriella's expressed fears, the dread she felt at the prospect of meeting the Aguilarez royals. Dammit—he should have told her who he was last night, offered reassurance. But once he'd realised she had no clue as to his identity, he had been unable to resist the opportunity to discover more about the real Gabriella Ross. He had little doubt she would have presented a very different side if she'd known the truth. Now at least he knew there was a spark of attraction, a base to build from. He'd sensed that from the moment he'd seen her sprawled in the straw; known with satisfaction, by the end of the moonlit ride, that the spark was mutual.

Anyway, there was no need for guilt; he had sent a letter of explanation so she wouldn't be taken by surprise. He suspected she'd be hopping mad but as a queen-to-be she would have to school herself to mask the emotion in public. Cesar did realise that a furious woman was not the best start to Campaign Marriage but his plan was to use the ball to advance a charm offensive.

'Cesar.' His sister's hiss pulled him back to the ballroom. Dignitaries and officials lined the walls, awaiting the all-important presentation that would indicate to the world that Meribel's actions and the arrival of a new ruler had not affected the alliance between Casavalle and Aguilarez.

His parents advanced slowly down the deep gold and blue carpet laid on the marbled floor towards where the House of Valenti awaited. Now Cesar's gaze was drawn unerringly to Gabriella and his breath hitched in his chest. The beauty that had poleaxed him the previous night was now on full display.

Her dress was an incredible concoction of elegance. Black and white, wide skirted, with an intricacy of lace and embroidered flowers over a white tulle. The straps were made of delicately shaped flowers that skimmed the creamy skin of her shoulders and Cesar's throat parched. Her chestnut hair fell in loose waves around a face of classic beauty, though he could see a shadow in her brown eyes, a tension in her smooth jawline. As she greeted his parents, he heard the murmur of her Canadian-twanged voice, the words a little breathless, a little rehearsed, the smile slightly strained, but overall she held up well and he found himself applauding inwardly. Next his brothers and now it was his turn.

Deep brown eyes raised to look at his face, the automatic greeting started, 'Welcome your…' then her voice trailed off, those brown eyes widened in shock and he realised in that instant that the letter had not reached her, decided that his hapless aide was toast. 'What are you doing h…?' Now her eyes narrowed as she put two and two together and he could see the anger dawn, heard the buzz of interest begin to hum round the room.

Cesar bowed. 'It is an honour to meet you, Your Royal Highness,' he said. It might be against protocol to interrupt but he knew it was better than allowing her to continue.

Gabriella looked down and then back up again and he could see the effort it took her to speak through no doubt gritted teeth. 'And you…it is a pleasure to see you here. I know your ambassadorial duties are heavy and I'm very happy that you were able to make it in honour of our countries' continued friendship.'

The words reeled off and only a slight flush on the angles of her cheekbones denoted her discomfiture as he moved on and she greeted Flavia. Cesar could only hope the damage had been limited, though he had little doubt the slip would be analysed, dissected and leaked to the gossip magazines worldwide.

Part of this was his fault, he knew, but Gabriella would need to learn to mask emotions and feelings if she was to survive the royal world.

'Cesar, what was that about?' His father's tone was cold, and with rueful grimaces his brothers melted from his side. 'The Princess looked less than happy to see you.'

'I believe she simply got confused, Father.'

'Please remember what was agreed.'

Ordered more like, Cesar reflected as he kept a filial smile on his face and accepted a glass of champagne from a passing waiter.

'You are to woo the Princess, not antagonise her. This marriage is important and we are trusting you to do the best for your country. As your mother and I did.'

And are you happy? The words withered on his lips—there was no universe where he could ask his parents that. They quite simply would not comprehend the question. To them it was an irrelevance—they had done what was right; it would have been unthinkable to do otherwise. Happiness didn't come into it. Oh, God—was this what he was doomed to? No. His marriage would be loveless but he would not let it be so cold and passionless and unfeeling. Couldn't live like that or ask anyone else to. *Easy words.* Once the knot was tied there could be no escape.

But there was no choice and his father was right. If he wanted to make this marriage possible *and*, more importantly, make it work, he did need to woo Gabriella; and he had to admit the courtship had not got off to the best start.

Time to regain lost ground and tread carefully on it; all eyes would be on them, watching every move. Gabriella was standing in a small group with Queen Maria and a couple of dignitaries, who she listened to with courteous interest.

He approached and, aided discreetly by Queen Maria, soon they were left alone, or as alone as it was possible to be at such a function. Her brown eyes glinted with anger but to her credit she managed a thin-lipped smile. 'Your Royal Highness. I hope you're enjoying yourself.' The words held more than a hint of bitterness. 'And my discomfiture.'

'Of course I am not enjoying your discomfiture, rather I would like to apologise for my part in this situation. I did send a letter of explanation but it appears you didn't receive it.'

'A letter?' Her voice was low, though her lips remained upturned. 'How thoughtful.' The sarcasm trembled her tone and as subtly as possible he manoeuvred them towards a garlanded pillar, hoping to shield her from view. 'It didn't occur to you to use something more…up to date? Like a phone. Or perhaps even turn up in person.'

'I was aiming at discretion.'

'Well, you missed your target.'

'Clearly. But here and now you have to do better than this. You need to look as if this conversation is enjoyable. People will have noticed that our greeting was strained.'

'I'm not an award-winning actress.'

'Then you need to learn. Fast. Part of being royal is an ability to wear a mask.'

'Well, clearly I am not royal enough. Why? Why didn't you tell me who you were?' She lifted a hand to her cheek. 'I am so angry and so mortified I could…'

'Could what?' His tone was low but harder now. 'Ruin everything you've worked so hard for? You told me this ball was important. For you and for your country. As it is for mine. If you don't want to blow this you need to pull it together. This is political now—if the public or the press believe we are fighting this will have ramifications on our two countries. Do you understand?'

Dear God, this was not going to plan but he needed her to get it and she did; he saw the understanding touch her eyes, watched her expression smooth to a semblance of serenity. She inhaled a deep breath and nodded. 'Fine. You're right. I understand.'

'Good. And, ma'am?'

'Yes.'

'I truly do apologise.'

She shook her head, but the smile on her face made the gesture appear casual. 'You let me make a fool of myself.' Now guilt touched him as he remembered again how worried she had already been about the evening.

'No! Gabriella. You didn't.' Without even meaning to he put a finger under her chin, tilted her face up so she looked directly into his eyes. And he saw the pain but also saw how hard she tried to conceal it. Remembered that until recently Gabriella Ross hadn't even set foot in Casavalle; she had not been brought up to mask emotions and play a role. And he had no right to expect her to.

He, Cesar Asturias, ambassador extraordinaire, had screwed up and now he needed to fix it. 'I swear it.' He would not have her undone for his own fault. So, 'Smile. Look at me as if you like me.'

'I'll try.' She sighed and the sheer weariness in that breath touched him, as he understood just how hard this was for her.

'You liked me yesterday. I am that same man.'

'No. You aren't. You are a prince, not an employee; you lied to me. Misled me, duped me, whatever term you wish to use.'

'I kept my identity from you and I truly apologise for that. It was a mistake. But everything else I said was true, was real. Think back to my words. None of them were lies. Not one.' He waited as she bit her lip, studied his expression.

'Not one?' she asked softly.

'No.' That he knew. 'I promise.'

Perhaps she heard the sincerity in his voice. In truth, for the past few minutes he had forgotten that they weren't alone, had wanted her to believe him with a fierceness that was out of proportion. Disquiet touched him and he dismissed it. It was vital he win her over, or the chances of her considering his suit were minimal. That explained the ridiculous swathe of relief when she gave a small nod and smiled a small but this time genuine smile.

'For the sake of this evening and for the man I met last night I will give you the benefit of the doubt. But I wish that letter of explanation had reached me.'

'Perhaps I could explain in person. Tomorrow. We could go for a ride.'

'I have engagements all day.'

'At the end of the day, then. We could have a picnic supper; leave the details to me. Meet me at the stables.'

As she hesitated, he suspected he knew the cause, knew he was right as he saw her lips twist half in rue, half in exasperation. 'I understand you need to check before you accept—that is part of royalty. Sometimes simple decisions have ramifications.' He also knew there would not be a problem. If she asked Queen Maria, consent would be granted—after all, Queen Maria had agreed this marriage would be a good one, though had stipulated she would not force Gabriella into it.

*'If it is the genuine wish of both, and they both be-
lieve they can have a happy life together, then and only
then will I believe that this will work.'*

Gabriella nodded. 'I'll confirm with you later. And
now I must mingle. I mustn't neglect my guests.'

'You are right. But remember the first dance is mine.'

Worry-laced panic now skimmed her expression and
without thought he took one of her hands in his, gave a
quick clasp of reassurance. 'I promise it will be a dance
to remember,' he said. 'And, Gabriella?'

'Yes.'

'I told you I didn't lie and I did not. When I told you
that Prince Cesar would be dazzled I was telling the
truth. You look beautiful and I am truly dazzled.'

Now she looked adorably confused, her nose crinkled
and her blush deepened. 'As if...' she muttered.

'I swear it. If there were not so many people watching I would prove it to you.'

'How?' Her voice was wary.

'I'd kiss you.' He smiled. 'Or I would ask permission to.'

'I... I... I...'

'What would you say?'

Suddenly she returned his smile; an impish dimple
appeared in her cheek. 'Why don't you try me and see?'
Clearly seeing that she'd wrong-footed him, she allowed
her smile to morph into a small triumphant chuckle and
he found himself laughing too. 'Now I really must mingle.' And with a look over her shoulder she glided away.

Had she really said that? Had she lost the plot along with
the royal rule book? Gabi resisted the urge to go and
hide behind a Christmas tree, to give herself a chance

to regroup and figure out what had just happened. But she couldn't; the royal ship needed to continue its regal sail. So she had to overcome the fluster and somehow rein in her thoughts, hide the tumult going on in her brain and her body.

Her mystery man was Prince Cesar Asturias and by rights she should be furious at his deception. Especially when he'd had the temerity to tell her *she* needed to pull *herself* together. Problem was he'd been right. She had been livid, hurt, angry, confused…and she'd been showing it. Royal rule number one: show no emotion.

And then somehow Cesar had got past her fury, because the apology in his brown eyes had been sincere and so too had been the glint of admiration. Dazzled, that was what he'd said. And that was all it had taken; she'd metaphorically melted into a puddle and flirted… practically promised to kiss him. Cue mental eye roll. Was she that much of a pushover?

Enough; she would banish Prince Cesar from her mind and focus on what she should be doing. Creating the right impression, making all these people believe she had it in her to rule.

And just like that the crushing weight of responsibility, the fear she'd mess this up, returned. The strangeness of wearing a ball gown, the unaccustomed shoes, the splendour of the room itself threatened to overwhelm her. But somehow she summoned the royal smile, the one practised in front of the mirror until her cheeks ached, as Queen Maria approached her, with yet another person by her side to introduce.

An hour later and, 'You OK?' She turned to see Luca at her side and she smiled, relieved to see her eldest brother, a man who understood all this.

'I'm fine, maybe a bit overwhelmed.'

'You're doing great.'

'At looking the part.'

He shook her head. 'This isn't about looking the part, or playing a part. You are a princess, Gabi, and you will be Casavalle's Queen.'

'That's what Cesar said.' Gabi regretted the words as she saw Luca study her expression.

'Sounds like you got to know each other fast.'

'Yes.' Gabi pushed away the urge to confide; the relationship between the Valentis and the Asturiases was complicated enough. She didn't need Luca to get involved or fire up on his sister's behalf.

'Well, he's right, Gabi. You can do this. You've got this.'

'Thank you. To you and Imogen. For having my back.'

'That's what family is for, Gabi. And now you have a family. To support you.' Luca smiled at her. 'So let's show some Valenti-Ross solidarity and build on what you have started with Prince Cesar. I have spoken with his older brothers and his younger sister already. Now let's go get some more publicity.'

Gabi nodded, understood the importance of this public meeting of the families. Luca had told her that a few months earlier he and Cesar had gone to see Meribel, and they had all made their peace. But that had been a private meeting; this was a public showing of togetherness, an assertion that neither family bore a grudge, that both families were friends.

He looked round. 'But let's bring Imogen into the mix too.' He smiled as his fiancée headed towards him, clearly alerted by some mysterious couple radar, and for a mad moment envy tinged with wistfulness touched

Gabi. She was happy for her best friend, for her brother, but she couldn't help but wonder if she could ever find what they had. Could she ever find love, trust that some-one would love her for herself?

'Let's do this,' Luca said. With smiles and murmurs to other guests they made their way through the glitter-ing, designer-clad throngs together and now Gabi felt lighter, revelled in the feel of being part of a family unit. Reminded herself that she did have support and backup and she was thankful for it.

They approached Cesar, who was speaking with Queen Maria, and Gabi gulped. Standing beneath one of the magnificent chandeliers, dressed in a tux that moulded his body, showed off those powerful shoulders and that lean, mean, fighting-machine body, he took her breath away. Again.

As if he sensed it, his dark brown eyes flicked to meet hers and she saw an answering flare there and her in-sides knotted in sudden desire. And she'd asked him to ask permission to kiss her. Madness—Cesar was not a man to flirt with; she might as well flirt with fire, dance and weave through the flames.

'Cesar. Good to see you.' Luca's deep tone was pitched to carry without shouting and Gabi was aware that around them conversations slowed as the two men shook hands. 'Much has changed since we last met,' he continued, with a disarming smile. 'I wish to assure you and your family that I for one have no complaint at all as to how things have played out. I am a very happy man. I have gained a sister and a fiancée I love. Gabri-ella you have met, but now allow me to introduce Imo-gen, my fiancée.'

'It is a pleasure to meet you, Imogen.' Now Cesar

grasped Imogen's hand, seemingly oblivious to the buzz around them. 'May I offer my sincere congratulations and wish you both happiness from myself and my family.'

'Thank you.' Imogen's voice was clear. 'I appreciate that very much. And please tell Meribel we wish her as much happiness as we have found.'

'I will do that.' Cesar's smile was courteous; he was clearly appreciative of Imogen's diplomatic answer. 'And may I say you will make a wonderful diplomat if ever the urge takes you.'

At that moment the band struck up and Cesar's smile changed, as if he'd upped the brightness meter, and he turned to Gabi. 'My dance, I believe.'

She would swear she could feel the colour leech from her face; she, Gabriella Ross, was about to lead a royal ball, a ball in her honour. Crazy didn't cover it.

'You'll wow them, Gabi,' Imogen said. 'And we'll be right behind you.'

'You'd better be.' Gabi turned to Cesar, oddly reassured—he would know what he was doing so with any luck she wouldn't make a complete fool of herself.

'There is no need to be nervous,' Cesar said softly as he took her hand and they approached the dance floor, where the orchestra had started the introduction, the melody touching and humming the air with motes of beauty.

'There is every need to be nervous. I told you last night, this is not my forte.'

'And I told you last night that you can do this. Plus what I didn't tell you last night is that I have all the moves!' As she glanced up at him, he did a disco move reminiscent of the seventies, the move so unexpected that she halted and looked up at him in surprise.

His face creased into a grin and he chuckled and she grinned right back. Suddenly the whole idea of the dance seemed less of an ordeal and as the orchestra began to play, she inhaled deeply. 'OK. I can do this.'

'We can do this,' he said and then they were off.

Gabi focused on his left shoulder, murmured the instructions under her breath, tried to focus on the movements, but it was hard when Cesar was this close. So close his aftershave tantalised her, so close she now knew the muscles were real, hard under her fingers; she could see one errant black curl on the nape of his neck and she bit back a small moan. The feel of his arm around her waist was ridiculously intimate as he guided her with a deft gentleness that made her shiver. And all she wanted was to be even closer; somehow it felt as though the rest of the room, the guests, the noise, had all faded away to leave only them…no one else.

Until the music came to its haunting close and she blinked as if emerging from a dream, became aware of all the other couples on the floor around them, suddenly conscious of the attention they had attracted. Oh, hell! She hadn't done anything stupid, had she? Drooled all over that beautiful tux, ripped open the jacket…

With as much dignity as she could muster, she managed a smile that she hoped looked cool but friendly. 'Thank you. Your moves helped a lot.'

This pulled a return smile, but his was way more than friendly and his gaze felt like a caress.

'Let me get you a drink,' he suggested. 'Before you take up your duties. There are many people who you must dance with tonight. But if we don't get a chance to speak properly again, I hope to see you tomorrow evening. We have much to discuss.'

They did? Gabi watched the breadth of his retreating back, turned to smile dutifully at the elderly gentleman, an English lord, who now approached her. But as she spoke with him her mind and her body dwelled on Cesar and anticipation twisted her tummy at the thought of their next meeting.

CHAPTER FOUR

COUNTLESS HOURS LATER and Gabi looked round the now empty reception room with a sigh of relief and eased her high heels off. 'That feels better.'

'Perhaps.' Queen Maria's voice held no censure, but it did hold a certain gentle implacability. 'But you need to keep the shoes on, Gabriella. It is possible that a guest will return, or a staff member enter—it would not look good for you to be seen barefoot, unprepared.'

Human... The thought entered Gabi's head as she slipped her aching feet back into the pointed, strappy, beautiful torture chambers. It would make her look human. Yet it didn't surprise her that there was a royal protocol that dictated a sight of the royal feet was taboo.

Maria reached out and placed a gentle hand on her arm. 'Thank you and you did well tonight.'

Gabi wasn't so sure; she knew she'd made mistakes, had knocked a glass of water over at the table and she was pretty sure she hadn't used the correct cutlery. All the while she'd been, oh, so aware of Cesar's presence; half of her had wished he'd been next to her, half of her relieved he wasn't. Instead she had spoken with his parents, wondered if she'd imagined the assessment in their eyes, the coldness behind the smiles. It was as if they saw the princess but not the person. But that was true of everyone. Except Cesar. Last night, this evening, he had treated her as a human being.

Now she glanced at her stepmother. 'Cesar asked me to meet him tomorrow evening.' A glance at the ornate grandfather clock in the corner of the room showed her the time. 'This evening,' she amended. 'I wasn't sure if I should or not?'

'Do you want to?' Maria's eyes met hers and to her annoyance Gabi felt a blush creep over her face.

'I'm not sure,' she settled for, which was no more than the truth. Part of her wanted to go, to satisfy her curiosity as to why he hadn't revealed his identity the night before. Part of her wanted to go because...

You want him to kiss you...that insidious voice whispered at the back of her mind.

No! No! No!

That was nuts. Because Cesar Asturias was not her type of man and no doubt he had simply been flirting with her out of...habit. The man had certainly dated his share of women, all far more beautiful than Gabi.

Maria surveyed her. 'There can be no harm in meeting him,' she said. 'It would show that the two royal families are friends; would demonstrate the Asturias family's acceptance of your position.' The Queen's expression held its usual serene inscrutability but there was something in her eyes, something elusive that Gabi couldn't read. 'But that can be done in public. I would not expect you to meet privately if you dislike him.'

'I didn't dislike him...' Now the flush deepened and clambered over her cheekbones. 'I... I think I'll meet him.' After all, she wasn't going to kiss him and she did deserve an explanation. And she would get to ride Arya again.

The Queen nodded. 'Now you should get some rest; it is a busy day tomorrow. You did truly well tonight.'

'Thank you.' Gabi knew praise did not always come easy to the other woman, that she expected a certain standard from her own sons and now from Gabi. But she knew too that she owed Maria so much. The Queen had shown no resentment towards Gabi, the woman who had usurped her own children's line to the throne. Instead she had gone out of her way to help her, guide her and advise her. On impulse Gabi moved over and gave the older woman a hug. 'And thank you for everything and the way you have welcomed me to Casavalle.'

For a second Maria froze, then she relaxed into the embrace, patted Gabi on the back before stepping back.

'It has been my pleasure. I see how Luca and Antonio have taken you to their hearts. And I know your father would have been proud of you.'

The words caused a lump in Gabi's throat: the familiar conflict of emotion. If only she'd found her mom's letters sooner, then she would have met her father. For a moment she brooded on the second letter, the one she had told no one about. The one where Sophia explained that she had wanted to return to Casavalle. Once Gabriella was born she'd realised she had been wrong to flee, that she loved her husband and wanted to work it out, that she wanted to take back her request for a divorce. But then she had discovered that Vincenzo had started seeing someone else, a suitable woman, someone who 'would be the wife I could never be', 'the wife Vincenzo needs' and so she had decided it would be better for everyone if she remained in Canada.

Now, as she looked at Maria, Gabriella vowed again never to reveal that letter, knowing it would hurt Maria, impact her memories of a successful marriage, make her play the game of if and but. Gabi knew now too that if the papers got hold of the information they would splash it around with glee, uncaring of who they hurt in the doing.

'Thank you,' she said. 'I so wish I could have met him, but I am so very grateful to you for everything.'

Knowing Maria would be super uncomfortable if she saw the tears that prickled the backs of Gabi's eyes, she smiled, blew the older woman a kiss and left the reception room. Hoped sheer exhaustion would allow her to fall into a dreamless sleep that did not feature Prince Cesar of Aguilarez.

And when they next met she would not be beguiled into flirting, would not be befuddled by the feel of his arms around her and there would be no observers so she would have no need of diplomacy. She would get an explanation for his behaviour.

As the sun set over the courtyard, Cesar crossed the mosaic paving to the Casavallian stables and nodded to the stable hand who was already at work saddling up Arya. He stroked the horse's nose and then opened Ferron's stall. 'I'll saddle up Ferron.'

Twenty minutes later the horses were ready and he led Ferron into the courtyard and saw Gabi approaching, in jeans and a short navy-blue padded jacket with a furred hood from which he could glimpse a glint of chestnut hair. And she looked as beautiful as she had in full ball regalia. But today her eyes held a combatant gleam, though her expression softened as she walked up to Arya and patted her neck.

'Good evening.'

'Hi.'

'I've arranged for a picnic to be brought to the maze.'

'The maze? Is that allowed? I thought it was about to be opened to the public.'

She mounted Arya with an easy grace, leant forward to pat the horse and murmur words in her ear.

'I've cleared it all with the palace gardeners, the Queen and anyone else I could think of. I thought it would be nice for you to see it in its festive beauty.'

As the horses trotted side by side he glanced across at her, tried to read her expression, but she seemed lost in thought and for a while he let the silence envelop them. Sensed that she was revelling in the evening sounds, the cold, crisp, dusky air, the puffs of breath from the horses, the orange red of the setting sun. In the silence after the hustle and bustle of the ball yesterday and her round of engagements today.

It gave him a chance to run over his strategy, the tactics necessary to win Gabriella. Again, today, his father had made his views clear.

'Make her fall in love with you, Cesar. Turn on the charm for which you are so famed.'

The idea had been endorsed by Queen Adriana.

'It is the best way. Gabriella is not like us; she will expect the more vulgar emotions.'

Anger had sizzled through him; Cesar did not believe emotions were a good thing but he wouldn't condemn them as vulgar. Neither would he lie to Gabriella; to trick her into falling in love with him with promises of an emotion he could not feel was dishonourable. And unlike his parents he did not believe that in this case the end justified the means. It would make for a disastrous marriage and also be an illusion that would be impossible to sustain.

Cesar hoped and fully intended to achieve his goal in a different way. Yes, he would use charm. Because charm worked. He'd figured that out as a child; it had been a survival strategy. The best way to win over the stream of royal nannies had been charm, cuteness with a soupçon of cheekiness. An acceptance that to them he was a job, not an object of love or affection. Acceptance that they moved on. Cesar could still feel the wrench in his gut he'd experienced when his first nanny had left. *Never again.* Oh, she'd been nice enough, had been sad to leave him, but she'd still gone. To have a family of her own. Lesson learnt. Charm the nannies to maximise their care of him; smile and the world smiled with you. A cliché that worked, even if sometimes the smiles were fake.

Perhaps now it was indeed time for a smile, time to start the charm offensive. He shot a quick glance at her, straight backed and poised on Arya's back. 'So, did you enjoy last night?' he asked.

'It had its moments.' A memory of their dance, how she had felt in his arms, shimmered in the air. 'But on the whole? Honestly?' Gabriella shook her head. 'I felt out of my depth and utterly exhausted. The things that come effortlessly to you, to Luca, are a struggle for me. I'm not used to being the centre of attention and I hate it. The idea that everyone is watching me makes me nervous.'

'You will need to get used to it.'

'I know.' The idea clearly was not one that filled her with joy and she gave her head a small shake as if to try and dispel the gloom. 'And I'm sure it gets easier. But it's not just the spotlight, it's the public interest; most mornings I read stuff about myself that is either malicious, or untrue, or taken out of context or is surely not of any interest. I mean, how can how I like my eggs be interesting?'

'The press is something you have to accept and in time you will learn to ignore the hurtful and preposterous. You will make connections with positive journalists and learn to use them to your advantage.' Another example of the way charm and making the best of a situation could be useful.

'I hope you're right.' As if hearing her own doubt, she shook her head again and then she frowned. 'But that's not what we're here to talk about. You're going to explain why on earth you didn't tell me who you were.'

'It's complicated.'

'I'd still like to know.'

'And I will tell you.' Deep breath here. 'When I walked into the stable I was annoyed, upset...'

'Why?'

Well, partly because he had felt the imminence of the metaphorical ball and chain, but that was not something he would share with Gabi. To tell her marriage was anathema to him would hardly prosper his suit and anyway that anathema was now irrelevant. Because he had accepted the necessity and he would make the best of it. 'Because I had not been consulted about the gift of Ferron and Arya,' he admitted, and was rewarded by a sympathetic smile. For a moment he felt a pang of guilt, which was foolish, as his words were truthful. 'Ferron was a particular favourite of mine.'

'I understand that and if you want I will gift him back. Happily.'

'That isn't necessary.'

'Then please know that whenever you wish to ride

him you can. But I still don't get why you didn't tell me who you were.'

'Well, my annoyance disappeared as soon as I saw a beautiful woman sprawled on the straw.'

Again true, and he derived a pleasure from seeing the flush on her cheeks, felt an immense gratitude that they were indeed true, that there was a genuine spark between himself and Gabi, a spark that he believed and hoped would make all the difference to their marriage.

'Fine words,' she said, 'but they don't answer the question. Unless you're going to try to spin me that my beauty gave you temporary amnesia?' The words were tart but with an undertone of honey and her lips curved upwards as she spoke, calling an answering smile from him.

'Would you believe me if I said that?'

'Nope. So, come on, no more sugared words.'

He raised a hand in acknowledgement. 'To begin with I assumed you would recognise me. Arrogant? Perhaps. But I thought that you would have been studying the Asturias family.'

Her sigh was deep. 'I did. I have. But...'

'I didn't stick in your mind?' He allowed mock chagrin to crease his face, put one hand on his heart as if wounded, and she grinned.

'Obviously not... But to be fair to me it was dark, secondly, I felt like a fool having been caught hiding in straw, third, I thought that there was no way Prince Cesar of Aguilarez would ever come into the stables.'

'Why not?'

'Because I didn't think the suave, sophisticated playboy ambassador would get his hands dirty.' Her eyes narrowed. 'Plus, I made the not unreasonable assumption that Prince Cesar would introduce himself. Not mislead me into believing he was a member of staff.' She pulled lightly on the reins, murmured to Arya and came to a stop. 'And you *still* haven't told me why.'

He too halted.

Deep breath. Choose your words carefully.

'I wanted to see what you were like. Really like. The real you.' The real her. The woman who had admitted to doubts and fears, the woman who had told him she would keep his words confidential, the woman he'd caught in his arms, the woman he'd desperately wanted to kiss. 'If I had told you who I was you would have been much more formal.'

'I'd also have been a whole lot more discreet.'

'Exactly. The whole political stance, the Asturias-Valenti relationship would have been a priority. I didn't want that. I wanted a chance to get to know you, without that layer.'

'Why?'

The million-dollar question. Looking round, he saw they were very nearly at their destination. 'Why don't we get some food…? And I will answer. I promise. First I want to show you this.'

Gabi realised she had been so absorbed in their conversation she had lost track of time and their surroundings. Now she realised that they would soon approach the maze, a truly incredible complex creation, the boxwood hedges dating back centuries.

But nothing had prepared her for how it looked this evening, in its Christmas splendour, and she gave a gasp of wonder. 'It's magical.' Gabi stared in utter delight. The twinkling lights had been woven and twisted into the verdant greenery to form an iridescent beautiful pattern of stars. Beautiful coloured lanterns lit the path leading to the maze, hung from the trees, each lantern a bauble of Christmas glittering beauty highlighted by the moon's beams.

'It's beautiful. Like a winter wonderland.' She frowned. 'We can't take the horses in, though.'

'No need. I've arranged for someone to meet us here and take them back to the stables. We will be picked up later.'

'You've thought of everything.' And it made her heart flutter. Because she knew he would have had to speak to a lot of people to get this set up just for them.

'I have tried. I want to show you that I am sorry for the unfortunate outcome of my deception. And I wanted you to see this.'

'Do you have anything similar in Aguilarez?'

'My country is more mountainous, craggier, less gentle; perhaps that reflects on our culture. But it is a magnificent country, a place that takes your breath away.'

'I would like to explore it.' Gabi could hear his love for his country in his voice, wondered then that he visited so infrequently. Of course his work kept him abroad but even so…

'Perhaps you will allow me to be your guide.'

Before she could reply, the sound of a car intruded and within minutes the large four-by-four had parked and a group of people climbed out. A few unloaded the boot and set off into the maze, whilst two youths headed towards Gabi and Cesar. As they approached both Ferron and Arya whinnied in recognition. Gabi dismounted, chatted to the newcomers and then watched as they mounted the horses and trotted off.

Cesar gestured towards the illuminated maze. 'Shall we? I do know the way but I am happy to wander round getting lost if you would prefer?'

Gabi sighed. 'I know the way too. There was a photo shoot; a publicity thing with Luca and I bonding by finding our way through the maze together.'

But, even with their knowing the way, the maze with its twisty wending turns and alleys was still both fascinating and breathtaking. Tucked into corners were wooden sculptures to depict a Christmas theme, elves, reindeer, robins all elaborately carved and placed for maximum effect. The lights twinkled and shone and glinted off the greenery and Gabi loved it.

'I love how Christmassy it all is. It sounds mad but I was so caught up with my presentation ball I'd almost forgotten how close Christmas is. Plus although the Casavalle palace is beautiful all the decorating is done by staff. I'm not complaining,' she said, quickly, 'but I'm used to decorating the book store myself.'

'I suppose this is very different from your usual Christmases.'

'Yes.' Gabi was silent for a moment. 'When I was a child Christmas was pretty quiet, but that was OK. Uncle Peter would get the tree and Aunt Bea and I always decorated it.' The memory was precious—it had been something the two of them could do together, a time where she'd felt a tenuous but real bond. 'We'd exchange a few gifts.' Always necessary items for Gabi, a new pair of shoes for school, a pair of gloves because her old ones had worn out, because that was always what she had asked for, not wanting to impose, always aware of what the elderly couple had given up for her both financially and emotionally. Their savings and their dream. 'After

Christmas dinner, we'd go for a walk.' There hadn't been much conversation but the silences had been companionable; it had been a time when she'd felt closest to them both. Gabi had always sensed she was accepted rather than wanted; when she was eight she'd understood why. An overheard conversation between Bea and a friend.

'She's a pretty little thing,' the friend had said and Gabi had beamed to herself. 'Sweet as well, polite.'

Then her Aunt Bea: 'I know she is and thank goodness for it. It was all a bit of a shock, really. Peter and I never wanted children and we had a plan for our retirement years. We were going to travel round Europe and end up in sunny Spain. Of course, we could never have done that once Sophia died. Gabriella is family and we would always do right by family. But sometimes I can't help but imagine how different life would be.'

Though her aunt and uncle had never told her of their thwarted plans, the words had haunted her for years, still caused a guilt that would tug at her for ever. She'd done her best to make it up to them, vowed to herself that somehow she would save enough so that one day they would still be able to travel. But it wasn't to be. Bea and Peter had passed away before that had been a possibility.

Gabi blinked herself back to the present, aware that Cesar was studying her expression, also aware of his words of the previous day—that royals should mask their feelings. And here she was, standing in a reverie of regret and guilt and haunted memories.

'Sorry. I got a little lost in the past. I bet your Christmases must have been a lot noisier than mine, with five siblings.'

'Noise wasn't encouraged in the royal household. Aguilarez does not embrace Christmas with the same verve as Casavalle. Or at least my parents do not. Our palace has one huge tree in the gardens for the public to see but we did not decorate inside like you do. Nor do we have anything like this maze.'

'So tell me about your Christmas Day.'

'We went to church, then we would visit the estate and we would open state gifts. The family didn't exchange gifts as we got so many from the public. We would send individual thank-you letters, of course—my parents believed it should be done by hand and done on Christmas Day.'

'At least you got loads of gifts.'

'We weren't allowed to keep them.'

'Why not?'

'There were too many and so my parents decreed none could be kept. So we donated them to charity.'

'That must have been really tough.' She frowned. 'But why didn't you exchange gifts, in that case?'

'Yes, we spotted that flaw.' Cesar shrugged. 'The general feeling was we were so lucky and privileged to be royal we didn't need gifts, I suppose. Christmas was more seen as an opportunity to give to the people than to celebrate in private.'

Gabi glanced at him. His voice was matter-of-fact. No anger or frustration, simple acceptance. And, she supposed, why should he complain? He was a prince, and he did have a fantastically privileged lifestyle. Yet he had missed out on the magical Christmases that were so important to childhood. Not because of the lack of gifts but because of the lack of Christmas spirit and family cheer.

'What about now?' he asked. 'How do you usually spend Christmas?'

'I kept the book store open so that people could come

and have some festive fare and some company. I realised there are a lot of lonely people out there. People on their own at Christmas. So I'd make some turkey sandwiches, *tourtière*, a Yule log, Christmas cookies and mulled cider and people could just drop in as they liked. I loved it.' Homesickness threatened and she blinked quickly, reminded herself again that royals didn't show emotions. 'What about you?'

'I tend to holiday at Christmas, sometimes skiing, sometimes tropical, always fun.'

No doubt the fun included a gorgeous girlfriend, but that was none of her business and before she could reply they arrived at the centre of the maze where Gabi halted. 'Oh, my goodness.'

The space had been transformed into a magical grotto. A wooden carved nativity scene made her catch her breath as she went over and examined the lovingly exquisite detail, marvelled at the talent that had created the small figures, the people and the animals, the cradle, the Virgin Mary, all somehow imbued with a sense of simplicity, grace and awe.

A table had been set up, covered in an embroidered damask tablecloth, laid with gleaming cutlery and starched napkins. The centrepiece was a magical burst of Christmas colours. Heaters had been set up to combat the wintry night air, and additional lights cast a golden illumination. The air was rich with the scent of food laid out on the table in a display that made her mouth water.

Three staff members were putting the finishing touches to the table. One approached them with a smile. 'Welcome. All is ready, Your Highness. The champagne is chilled, the picnic is laid out. I hope you both enjoy the food.'

With that, all the staff melted discreetly away and Gabi stared in delight at the tableau. 'This is what you call a picnic?'

'Yup. Picnic Cesar Asturias style.'

'Impressive. It's beautiful.' And her heart gave a hop, skip and jump. *Whoa.* Keep this real, Gabi. You may be nearly Queen, but you're still Gabi Ross, gawky book nerd. Not Cesar's type of woman at all. This was a political gesture, nothing more.

Cesar pulled a chair out and Gabi sat down, waited for him to seat himself opposite her. He looked impossibly handsome and for a moment her head whirled. *Focus.* Instinct told her that perhaps this was more than a gesture. This was a man schooled in diplomacy, a man whose every word and action were no doubt dictated by policy.

'Thank you,' she said as she accepted a crystal flute brimming with champagne, lifted it in toast. 'To answers,' she said. 'Speaking of which, I'd like some. What is all this about? What was the night we met about? Why was it so important to get an impression about the "real" me?'

He helped himself from a bowl of pasta salad, the shapes gleaming with oil, dotted with olives, capers and cubes of a tart, local cheese, and studied her across the table, his dark eyes thoughtful, his expression neutral, the only sign of tension the tautness of his jaw.

'I'm Canadian as well as Casavallian,' Gabi reminded him. 'We favour the direct approach. There is no need to be diplomatic here. I'd rather you cut to the chase and told me.'

A shrug and, 'OK.' He nodded. 'I wanted to see if there was a compatibility between us. Because I believe we should consider a marriage.'

'Whose marriage?' The stupidity of the question was apparent to her even as she spoke the words. Yet surely he couldn't possibly mean...

'Our marriage.'

'You and me? You think *we* should get *married*?' Panic threatened and she shoved her chair back; her fork fell with a clatter onto the china plate. 'One waltz and a sip of fizz and you are proposing?'

Cesar rose to his feet. 'Hold on. It is not a proposal. It is an idea for us to discuss. To consider as a possible future option.'

'I think you'll find that is the *definition* of a proposal. I don't need to consider it. I need to leave. Now.' She stood up. Was she overreacting? Gabi gave it a couple of seconds' consideration and decided not.

He inhaled deeply. 'Please stay. Tell me why you won't consider it?'

Gabi opened her mouth and then closed it again. There were so many reasons, all so incredibly obvious to her. 'Why *would* I consider it?'

'For Casavalle. For Aguilarez. For our countries.'

The words, in their simplicity, echoed round the glade, caromed off the dark evergreen leaves, magnified and filled the air. Gabriella fought the urge to turn and run from the weighted knowledge that her life was no longer her own to live. Instead it belonged to her country.

'You know our countries' histories,' he continued.

'I do, and I know that in the past the enmity was deep and bloody. But there has been peace for over two centuries.' Which surely meant the whole need for a marriage was ludicrous.

'Yet right now the situation is precarious. There are still many who feel it is foolish for one small island to have two countries, two royal families. Others think royalty should be replaced by democracy. Right now even royalists are unhappy. Many in Casavalle feel that Meribel has insulted the House of Valenti, many in my country feel Luca should have backed out, that he would have married Meribel under false pretences.'

'And there are also those who believe that I am a usurper and that Luca is the rightful King.' Gabriella sighed. 'Perhaps I made a mistake. Perhaps I should just stand aside, allow Luca to fulfil the destiny he was brought up to, take the throne.'

Cesar shook his head. 'You cannot put the genie back in the bottle, Gabriella. You are the rightful heir; you are King Vincenzo's oldest child.'

'I know. I have been through it all in my head so many times. Luca, Antonio and Maria all believe I should take the throne.'

'I too agree with this. Both countries must unite behind a position: the honourable one, the right one. Our marriage would represent that union.'

'I am sure our countries would survive without our marriage,' she said, her fingers tight round the back of her chair.

'Of course, they would.' The deep voice was full of reassurance. 'Please, sit down. Let me explain. I am not trying to force you into a course of action you do not want. I cannot do that even if I wished it. But I believe this is an idea that would benefit both our countries.'

An insidious tendril of disappointment snuck through her; she'd thought…thought what? That Cesar liked her, was attracted to her, was interested in her. Well, the last at least was true, though not for the reasons she'd naively, foolishly hoped. She was royalty now, soon to be

Queen, and she needed to get real. Cesar Asturias had been linked to numerous beautiful, sophisticated women in his time...he wouldn't have given Gabi a second look if it weren't for her crown.

But at least he had had the courtesy to be honest and in return royal manners dictated that she listen to him. *Then* she could tell him to shove it.

So she sat down, right on the edge of her seat. 'OK. Explain.'

CHAPTER FIVE

WITH AN ABILITY born of years of top-level diplomacy Cesar didn't let the relief show on his face, tried not to show the fact that he was rattled. This was not going according to plan at all. Perhaps his insistence that Queen Maria not interfere, not lay the groundwork had been a mistake, but he'd been convinced that this agreement had to be between himself and Gabriella. Her decision not tainted or influenced by either his family or hers.

'First, I'm sorry—I thought that maybe given the fact that Luca was meant to marry Meribel, you would perhaps have considered an alliance through marriage between our countries.'

'Given how that worked out it is hardly surprising I didn't,' she pointed out and he had to admit the point was valid. 'If that marriage had never been considered it would have been way easier for everyone.'

'Easier isn't always right.'

'Do you believe they should have gone through with it?'

'No. I don't. Foisting a fake heir onto Casavalle would have been a disaster. That scandal would have been even worse than the scandal of leaving Luca at the altar. I believe that Meribel should not have allowed herself to get into the situation she did.'

'I don't know exactly what happened. But perhaps Meribel fell in love—how could she have prevented herself from doing that?'

'She could have closed it down as soon as she felt anything for Dana. People don't just fall in love in an instant.' And yet...he remembered the look on his sister's face when she had spoken to Luca. Tears had slid down her cheeks as she'd admitted the guilt she felt over how she had treated him, brought shame to her house. But when Meribel had declared her love for the father of her baby, for Dana, her face had glowed with a belief and a certainty and he'd known that his sister had changed. Would go to the wall for this love. *Stupidity.* Though Luca seemed to have understood.

'Yes, they do,' Gabriella said. 'Look at Luca and Imogen; they certainly didn't mean to fall in love. Neither did Antonio and Tia. But they did. Antonio and Tia are getting married in a few days; their baby is due in a couple of months.'

'And I wish them every happiness.'

'But...?' There was a challenge in her voice.

But their pursuit of happiness had resulted in Cesar having to take a forced march to the altar. As far as he was concerned Meribel... Luca... Antonio had all lost the royal plot, leaving him and Gabriella to put events back on track. *It is as it is, Cesar. Make the best of it.* The Cesar Asturias motto.

'But I don't believe that is the only way to find happiness, especially for royalty, especially for rulers.' In truth he didn't buy the whole love gig, the whole head over heels, giddy, goofy idiocy. 'Royals don't live normal lives and I don't think love does conquer all. And I don't think it can necessarily survive exposure to royal protocols and pressures.'

A shadow crossed her eyes again and he knew the words would have reminded her of her mother. 'I am sorry to cause you pain but…'

'But my parents' love didn't survive.' Her voice was flat, her expression guarded. 'My mother fled those protocols and pressures.'

'Yes,' he said simply. 'I do not blame her or accuse her. I understand how hard it must have been for her at a court full of unfamiliarity, where emotions had to be hidden and stifled and masked. I do not judge her, but I think it sensible to learn from her, from your parents. That perhaps sometimes the way to happiness is not through love.'

'But you don't want to marry me for the sake of happiness,' she said softly. 'You want to marry me to forge an alliance between our countries.'

'Yes. Yet I believe it could still be a happy alliance.'

'Why? How?'

Now he smiled, wanting to make her frown disappear, wanting to chase away the memories that shadowed her brown eyes. 'Well, for a start I'm part of the package and I am well known for my charm and wit and brilliance.' Her gaze met his with a startled expression and his smile broadened as he nodded. 'I am what is known as a catch.'

'You forgot an attribute,' she said.

'What's that?'

'Your endearing sense of modesty.'

That pulled a chuckle from him. 'Hey, if you don't believe in yourself, who will?' He reached out, covered her hands in his own, felt a thrill at the softness of her skin. 'But in all seriousness, I do believe we could make a go of it; I think we have something to build on.'

'What's that?' She looked down at their clasped hands and he knew his touch affected her as much as it did him.

'This,' he said softly. 'This spark; I felt it from the moment I saw you.' He gave a small shrug. 'And I know you feel the same way.' He grinned. 'I realise how arrogant that sounds but we've established I have no sense of modesty.'

'I…' Gabi shook her head. 'You can't decide to get married just because there is a spark. Sparks can go out.'

'Sparks can also be ignited into flames that can be stoked and nurtured, a fire that can continue to burn. I believe our spark is that kind of spark—and I promise I will do all I can to make that happen.'

Her eyes widened now and he saw desire and doubt in them. 'Let me show you. You said to me yesterday that I should ask your permission to kiss you. I ask that now.'

There was a slight quiver to her low laugh. 'You're offering me a taster, a sample?'

'I'm offering you proof this spark has life to it, that it will not fizzle out.'

She took a deep breath. 'Then… I grant my permission.'

Gently, his breath catching in his throat, he lifted one hand, gently stroked the crease that lined her forehead, ran his thumb over the fullness of her lower lip and heard her small intake of breath with deep satisfaction, a visceral reaction that stoked his need, a need becoming more primal, more necessary by the second.

He leant forward, his heartbeat accelerated, then his lips met hers, and he tasted the linger of spices, the tang of champagne and all that mattered was the surge of sensation, the drumbeat of desire. All he'd intended was a simple brush of the lips but her small groan undid him and he deepened the kiss, felt desire twist his gut as her fingers tangled in his hair and she matched him passion for passion.

The sound of a bird's long drawn-out call pulled him back to reality and gently he broke the kiss and they stared at each other. As their ragged breath mingled, a sense of panic assailed him.

Because suddenly the momentum hit him with a whoosh. If all went to plan that would be the first kiss of a lifetime of kisses; he would never kiss another woman again. The idea was huge. Not because he questioned his ability to be faithful, but because this made it real. Not an idea, not a political or diplomatic exercise, but a proper flesh and blood union.

A sudden image of his parents forced its way to his brain, soured the moment. Their relationship had been a political alliance and whilst they had had five children their union had yet been devoid of any sense of passion or joy. It had been founded on duty and evolved no further. And so Cesar had promised himself to eschew marriage and opt for the fun and passion of light hearted affaires.

Now here he was headed towards the altar. But this marriage would not be like his parents'—that kiss had shown him that. And for that he was suddenly immensely grateful—his emotions see-sawing by the second.

Wait a minute. Emotions? See-sawing?

He needed to relax. Gabi was looking at him, her eyes wide with a mixture of shell shock and vulnerability and muted desire.

Think, Cesar.

Before the silence stretched too long, before he succumbed to the overriding urge to kiss her again. The idea of losing control was not congenial—after all, this was a marriage campaign and that meant he had to be *in* control. Digging deep into his reserves of charm, he managed a smile, one of his best, used when it behoved him to epitomise Prince Charming.

'So did the sample pass muster?'

Now her expression changed, cooled, and she looked down, almost absent-mindedly dabbed her finger onto the crumbs on her plate. Then raised her head and her gaze met his, almost amused as she nodded.

'Yes, you passed. Well done,' she said. 'The spark box is now ticked. However, obviously there are still a lot more boxes to go. You can't build a marriage on one kiss.' Now she was arranging the crumbs in a line. 'What about us?'

Now it was his turn to frown. 'Us?'

'Yes. Us. Two human beings. You are proposing we get married, live together, have children, commit to each other.' The words in their enormity caused a small shudder of panic to ripple his body, one he quelled instantly. 'Yet I don't know you. You don't know me. And that doesn't seem to matter to you.'

'I know this must be hard for you to understand as a concept. But it is what we were brought up to accept as the norm. Marriages made for reasons other than love.'

'But it's so impersonal. You want to marry the Casavallian Queen—not me, Gabriella Ross.'

He drummed his fingers on his thigh. 'But Gabriella Ross is the Queen of Casavalle.'

'That's semantics and you know it. If I were still Gabi Ross, book-store owner, you wouldn't be proposing marriage.'

'No, I wouldn't.' There was no point dressing this up. 'But you aren't.'

Her forehead creased in another frown and she narrowed her eyes at him. 'I get that. My point is you would be proposing to whoever was sitting this side of the table.' Abandoning the crumbs, she pushed her plate away, picked up her glass and sipped the champagne. 'You would have set this up for any woman, kissed any woman, regardless of who she was as long as she was the next ruler of Casavalle.'

'No.' Now Cesar shook his head. 'That is not true. I set this up for you. I wanted you to see the maze in all its Christmas magic, I wanted to ride here at sunset with you. And I definitely wanted to kiss you.'

'But you would have tailor-made a different evening for a different woman.'

'Perhaps. But at the end of the day this is about you and me.'

She shook her head. 'This is about the Prince of Aguilarez and the nearly Queen of Casavalle. Not about Cesar and Gabi. As I said, you would never have proposed to Gabi Ross, book-store owner.'

'No.' Again there was no point in muffling the reality of their situation. He kept his gaze on hers. 'But I would have been attracted to you. I would have wanted to kiss you. The spark between us—that is real, that is between you and me. Gabi and Cesar. And that is important.'

'There are other things that are more important,' she said.

'I agree. And I realise I have sprung this idea on you, that you need time to process it. All I ask is that you consider what I have said today.'

'I promise I will think about it.'

'I can't ask more than that.' Indeed he couldn't. He topped up their glasses and raised his. 'To good thoughts,' he said. 'Now let us finish our meal—the selection of desserts is amazing. We can eat them in the moonlight and simply talk about other things. And then I will escort you home.'

The next morning, seated in the splendour of the palace library, her favourite room in the whole palace, the one where she felt most at home, Gabi prepared herself for her usual morning routine. A cup of tea by her side, curled up in an ornate overstuffed armchair, newspapers and netbook on the table in front of her, she fervently hoped that an imposition of normality could somehow balance out the surrealism of the previous evening. Cesar Asturias wanted to marry her. Cesar Asturias had kissed her. Gabi closed her eyes as her entire body tingled at the memory.

Enough. That kiss had meant nothing to Cesar—it had been a sampler, a proof that their marriage would contain a spark. He would have kissed any woman like that—he was an expert after all. Though just after, for an instant she would have sworn his eyes held a look of shock that no doubt mirrored her own. But then he'd blinked and she'd decided she must have imagined it.

Especially when he'd smiled the slow, satisfied smile of a man who knew he'd scored a winner. Which was when reality had doused her like a downspout of freezing water—the kiss might have been completely outside Gabi's experience…but not out of his.

Cesar Asturias was a man with a whole lot of experience in the kissing department, and she would not let herself be manipulated into marriage based on one expert lip lock.

In which case perhaps she should stop thinking about the damn kiss, and brace herself for her morning dose of the headlines.

Two minutes later she gave a muffled shriek as she absorbed the words, stared at the newspapers' headlines, at the netbook screen open to the celebrity pages. Shock rippled through her.

Royal Romance in the Air?
Could This Be Love?
A Private Picnic?
Diplomacy or Dalliance?

The accompanying photographs were even worse. Pictures from her presentation ball. Her and Cesar in conversation, her expression fierce. Then that waltz, her face tipped up with an intent look, as if her life depended on him. Then the actual article, nauseating paragraph after paragraph of speculation as to how a rocky start had led to a dance of dreaminess.

Then there were pictures of the picnic hampers being driven to the 'rendezvous'.

Sources confirm a romantic supper 'à deux' was requested by the clearly besotted Prince.

Besotted. Ha! When she got her hands on the 'sources' she would—

At that moment there was a knock on the door, it swung open and one of the palace staff entered. 'His Royal Highness Prince Cesar of Aguilarez,' he intoned.

Ah…the besotted Prince himself, looking anything but.

'Thank you, Leo.' She waited until the staff member had gone and then, 'Have you seen these?' she demanded.

'Yes. I came straight over so we can discuss a publicity strategy.'

Gabi looked at him open-mouthed. 'A strategy? How about complete outright denial?'

'That is one option,' he agreed.

'I sense that you have other preferred ones.'

'That depends.' He came further into the room, sat opposite her and despite her horror at the headlines she couldn't help her body's awareness of his proximity, that strange ripple in her tummy his presence caused. 'On what you have decided after our discussion last night.'

It was a question she had tussled with for most of a sleepless night, thoughts whirling in a restless vortex around her brain, interspersed with vivid images of their kiss. Because whilst Cesar was the epitome of the handsome prince and he had her hormones in a twirl... she had to remember that this was not a book, not a classic romance or a fairy tale. This was real life. Her life, his life, and scarily the decisions they made now would impact on the politics and well-being of their two countries as well as themselves. Eventually as she'd dropped into a doze as the dawn light had crept through the windows, she had come to a decision. 'I *had* decided that there would be no harm in discussing the matter further, rather than dismissing it out of hand.'

'Good. Then there is another viable strategy to deal with these articles. Apart from denial.'

'Such as?'

'We go along with it.'

Gabi blinked, tried to modulate her voice, tried to

keep herself from grabbing him by his broad shoulders and shaking him. 'And why would we do that?'

'Because these articles are feel good; they are positive—there is a tacit acceptance that you are royal, there is no mention of scandal, usurpers, pregnancies, jilted at the altar. All that is positive.'

Gabi stared at him and her eyes narrowed. 'Anyone would think you'd planned it yourself. Did you "leak" any of this; are you the "source" quoted?'

'I didn't plan it, but I didn't stop it either.'

Fabulous. 'So you have tacitly encouraged these fluffy, sickly, completely incorrect stories?' Unable to help it, she started to pace—perhaps she should be being suitably royal and poker-faced, but tough.

'Yes. I could have shut it down. I chose not to. Because I prefer to have a certain level of control of the stories, otherwise the press can pretty much make it up.'

'So instead you have made it up?'

'Yes. And I think we should continue to do so.'

'But it is insane. Surely they can't believe what they are writing. They must know that we barely know each other.'

'They are writing to sell their publications and people like romance. They want to believe the fairy tales. Think how they work out. The prince fits a glass slipper onto a mystery girl's foot and they live happily ever after. The prince fights through brambles, kisses a sleeping princess he has never even met because she has been asleep for a hundred years and they live happily ever after. People like stories like that. They almost see us royals as fictional characters, so why not provide a feel-good story?'

'Because we aren't fictional. We're real. And newsflash…we may *not* get married. In fact the chances of us getting married are marginally marginal. And even if we do there won't be any fluffy romance, any glass slippers. No fairy-tale ending.'

'But we can give an illusion of romance whilst we decide what we want to do. This kind of press is good publicity. Good for both our countries. It will distract attention away from all the scandals. We are planning to spend some time together getting to know each other; we can manage the publicity. Use it to our advantage.'

'So you think we should encourage the press to speculate that there is "romance in the air" whilst we spend time together figuring out if we want to make a cold-blooded alliance.'

'Not cold-blooded, no,' he said softly.

And there was that ripple of attraction. Again. To her relief a timid knock at the door was followed by the entrance of another of the palace staff, pushing a laden trolley in. 'Leo asked me to bring refreshments, ma'am.'

'Thank you, Donna,' Gabi said, waited as the young woman busied herself arranging the tea things on the table, caught the quick speculative glance she threw at Cesar before she left.

Cesar waited for the door to click shut and then, 'For example, we could have used that opportunity to give the impression of romance, let the spark show a little— then Donna would take that story back to the kitchen staff and that's how rumours grow.'

'Let the spark show.' Gabi closed her eyes in disbelief. 'Right now I'm not sure whether to be pleased or horrified that a spark exists at all, so the idea of deliberately flaunting it in public doesn't fill me with joy.'

'Flaunting is too strong a word,' he said blithely. 'The occasional look, the brush of our hands, a hand on the arm…no more than that, nothing that detracts from royal dignity. But to create an illusion, you have to live the illusion.'

Gabriella stared at him. 'You make it sound so easy.'

'It will be easy. The attraction exists—there will be no need to act. Do not look so worried. It will be like the waltz—we will pull it off.'

Like the waltz. The memory of his arms around her, the feel of his body next to hers…the attraction existed all right.

As he poured her a cup of tea, he raised his eyebrows as his hand hovered over the milk jug and he glanced at her in question.

'Just black, please. It's rooibos, one of my favourites.' Gabi gave a small laugh. 'For heaven's sake, you don't even know how I take my tea, but you want to marry me.'

'But after today I will know. We will learn about each other. And if we decide we will not suit then so be it. But in the meantime, I believe the romance strategy works. What do you think?'

Gabi tried to focus, to consider her options. She and Cesar were going to spend time together regardless; they couldn't tell the press the truth as to why and there would be speculation whatever they did. So… 'Fine. I'll do it.'

'Excellent. I will coordinate the publicity with your palace secretary.'

'Sure.' All of it was suddenly overwhelming and as she sipped her tea the taste was so very evocative of her book store, of her former life, that she felt a sudden threat of tears, closed her eyes to try and blink them away.

'Hey. Are you OK?' She heard the clink of a cup being placed down, felt his approach and opened her eyes as he squatted down in front of her chair.

'I'm sorry. I just had a wave of homesickness; a yearning to be sitting in my book store with a book and a cup of tea, chatting to customers, or students.' Back to her safe, ordered world. She kept talking, as much to distract herself as anything else. 'The book store was more than a job—it was like my home. My aunt and uncle bought it when I was young.' The all too familiar guilt hit her again. They had used the savings they had planned to spend on their adventurous retirement and they had run the store competently, but without passion. But it had been different for Gabi. For her the shop had been magical. 'I grew up in it and I always loved it. Loved the books, the smell of them, the feel of them and the sheer magic of them. I could literally escape into them. Live a different life, befriend the fictional characters.' She broke off. 'Sorry. I get a bit carried away.'

'That's fine. It's nice to see. Even if I don't get it.'

Gabi frowned. 'You must get it a bit. Think of your favourite book.'

This was greeted by silence.

'I do not read.'

'Excuse me?' Gabi put her cup of tea down and leant forward.

'Well, obviously I read reports and official documents and I read the news. Religiously. But if you mean books, fiction, poetry, then, no, I do not.'

'OK. But what about a childhood book? Once you learnt to read didn't you sit under the bedcovers with a torch, reading? You must have read something? Books about wizards? Books about princes? You must have read, or surely your parents read you bedtime stories.'

That was something she knew Sophia had done, one of the few snippets her aunt had let fall. And if she tried really hard Gabi was sure she remembered, had a faint elusive memory of a soft, modulated voice, reading, making farm-animal sounds, singing softly at bedtime. Her mother, barely remembered except as an almost dream, hard to distinguish between what she had imagined in her grief and sadness and how much had been real.

'No.' His brown eyes shadowed. 'None of the above. I did read the history of our countries, and there were some local authors that I was told to read from time to time. But fiction was seen as unessential.'

Gabi stared at him and he gave a sudden chuckle. 'You look absolutely horrified.'

'I am utterly horrified. How can you exist without reading? It doesn't have to be classic literature—it can be anything at all. But reading…it's a means of escape.' And you could do it anywhere. Reading had saved her as a child; allowed her to escape the knowledge that she was a burden. 'And it's enjoyable and…to me it's necessary.'

'So you think I should read?'

'I think everyone should read.'

'That's a little dictatorial.'

'Nope. It would be dictatorial if I chose their reading material. Everyone likes different things, different genres, different authors. Some people really can't take to fiction, others may only like short stories. Then there are biographies and information books and history books and I guess for some people a technical book will float their boat or…' She paused, waved her hand expansively. 'You get the picture. What I mean is everyone should be encouraged to read. Especially in this world of technology, it's important. For kids and for…' She stopped—what was she doing? Waffling on about books to a man who had made it clear that nothing was more important than duty to one's country, a man willing to pull the strings of the press, marry in the name of duty. Did Gabi spending time reading help her people, further her country's purpose? No, it didn't.

'Anyway,' she said. 'Sorry. I guess once a book-store owner, always a book-store owner.'

'I think I can see why you were so successful at it. You're clearly passionate about books.' He smiled. 'Your whole face lights up and your enthusiasm—it is infectious.'

'I *am* enthusiastic. I ran a store, ran literacy classes, and a book club. But now my life has changed.'

'That doesn't take away from everything you achieved.' As if he could hear the sadness in her voice he stepped towards her. 'I would have loved to see it, your book store, your former realm. To have met you whilst you were that person, but that person is still a part of you. The past doesn't just vanish…it makes us who we are today. Your reading, everything you got from books, everything you learnt from building up a business you love, you'll use all that. You really will.'

'Thank you.' The words made her feel better, made her feel as if her past life was important, rather than being swallowed up by this whole new world. 'I hope so.' She glanced at him a little shyly. 'I did think that maybe I could open this library up. Redesign it to make it more accessible to staff—not force anyone to come and read, but maybe simply offer access? I could get lots of tables, comfy chairs, drinks machines and obviously catalogue the books. Put the valuable ones up high, get a better mix of authors in…' She shrugged, clocked the intensity of his dark brown eyes. 'Or is that a stupid idea?'

'I think that's a great idea.'

'You do? Really?'

'Really. I don't say things I don't mean, Gabriella.' She could see his sincerity and it warmed her, as did his toe-curling smile.

'And now why don't you start with me?' he said.

For a minute she had no idea what he meant. Start with him how? Perhaps she could move forward, lift her hand, touch his cheek, move her hand down and cover the beat of his heart, stand on tiptoe, brush her lips against his…

Bad idea. That box was ticked; kissing him again would mess with her head, fuzz her brain, to say nothing of pandering to his ego. And that wasn't what he meant anyway, she realised as she saw him turn to scan the bookshelves.

'I would like you to choose me a book,' he continued.

Gathering herself together, she looked round at the shelves. 'A book?' she echoed.

'Yes. You have shown me how important books are to you—I would like to try and understand that.'

The idea touched her; perhaps all he could offer was an alliance, but at least he was trying and she appreciated that. 'OK. That sounds good.' A few moments' thought and she headed over to a corner of the room. 'This is where I've put my keeper shelf. Here, try this and this.' The first a book she was sure he'd love, an incredibly clever account of the life of a centenarian, and second, 'This is a book I've read and reread all my life. A Canadian classic—the story of a red-haired girl.' An orphan like herself.

Reaching out, he accepted the books and she forced herself not to react as his hand brushed hers; told herself it was scientifically impossible to have such heightened sensitivity that the fleeting contact triggered a shiver over her skin.

'Thank you,' he said.

'I hope you enjoy them, but if you don't that's fine too. There are plenty of others I can suggest.' Resisting the urge to reach out and grab his hand, to put scientific theory to test, she reminded herself of why Cesar was here. 'We seem to have got distracted—what happens next? With us?'

'I suggest we go on a date.'

'A date? So, like a fake date?' Visions of being paraded in front of the press filled her brain. 'How would it work?'

'Leave it to me. What is your schedule today?'

Gabi checked her netbook diary, showed the screen to Cesar, who scanned the timetable and grimaced. 'Is this a sample of a typical day?'

Gabi nodded. 'There is so much to learn.'

'There are different ways to learn,' he said. 'I will pick you up at twelve; you are supposed to be studying.'

It was time she set aside to studying Casavallian history, wanting to learn as much as she could about her country, the country she would soon rule over.

'Leave it all to me,' he declared. 'Just dress up warm.' Now his smile would melt the polar ice caps and she felt her toes curl. 'And don't look so worried. A date with me is not an ordeal. I promise.' Now his voice was a low, deep melted-chocolate rumble that slid over her skin. 'The idea is to have fun.'

Fun. Surely that was a good thing, right? As long as she kept her head, remembered the date part was a show for the press. Yet unwanted anticipation sizzled her veins. Giving up, she smiled back. 'I'll wear my favourite toque.'

CHAPTER SIX

GABRIELLA WAS TRUE to her word. At twelve exactly she entered the reception room with a red and white striped woollen hat sitting jauntily atop her head; she wore a red fleece-lined coat over jeans. And worry in her eyes.

'I take it the press are waiting outside.'

'Yes, but it'll be fine,' Cesar said. 'Trust me. We only have to face them for a few minutes tops until we get to the car. And your hat..."toque", was it?...it will bring you luck. Come.' Without thinking, he held out a hand and when she put her hand in his, he felt a sudden warmth. Hand-holding was not something he did—too cosy, too intimate... Belatedly he reminded himself it would look good for the cameras, felt a jangle of discomfort that that hadn't been his motivation. Enough. 'Ready?'

She nodded and he pushed the door open and they walked hand in hand towards the car, a security detail between them and the pack of reporters.

'Where are you going, Princess?'

'Is it a date, Cesar?'

He smiled easily, but said nothing as the door to the car was held open for them and Gabriella slid in.

Once in the car, he directed the driver to, 'Go, Roberto.'

Gabi turned. 'Won't they follow?'

'I'm counting on it.' He met her gaze. 'Relax, Gabriella—as I said, this will be fun. I promise.'

'OK. I'll try. Maybe you should tell me where we are going.'

'But that would ruin the surprise.' Anticipation curved his lips at the prospect of seeing Gabriella's face when she saw the venue of their date. He wanted to see her smile; knew that the headlines had worried her, knew that the prospect of marriage must be preying on her mind. 'I will give you a hint. I am taking you to Aguilarez.' He gestured to the window. 'Perhaps you can consider this to be a geography lesson. If you watch you will see how the landscape changes; the countryside becomes craggier, more mountainous. Harder. In terms of history sometimes I believe it shows the differences in our cultures, as I told you at the maze.' Gabriella turned to look, continued to study the countryside, the towns and villages as their journey progressed. Cesar took the opportunity to study her, the classical beauty of her features, the regal straight back, the gloss and shine of her hair.

After a while she turned to face him. 'I see what you mean. It is very different from Casavalle.'

'And I believe the difference in geography has impacted on our countries' histories,' he said. 'On Aguilarez crops were harder to grow, conditions were harsher, tougher and that meant my people either resented or looked down on your people who enjoyed better harvests and an easier lifestyle. So unrest began and grew into full-scale war. At other times it was Casavalle who was the aggressor—wanting to rule the entire island, to get rid of the constant need for defence, the constant threat.'

'And now?'

'Now modern technology, worldwide trade, imports

and exports, tourism, the treaties and agreements made by our ancestors have meant we are both prosperous countries and allies. Yet...'

'You still believe that alliance to be fragile.'

'It is difficult. As children my brothers used to play with toy soldiers and the opposing armies were from Aguilarez and Casavalle. One day my oldest brother will be King and my next brother is rising the ranks in the army, as was ordained from birth.'

'And you? What did you do as a child?'

'I tried to broker a truce—after all, even then I knew diplomacy was my future.'

'What would have happened if you hadn't wanted to be a diplomat? What if you'd decided you wanted to be a surgeon or a banker or a teacher or...?' She broke off. 'You get the picture.'

Cesar shook his head. 'It didn't work like that in our families. Some options, most options weren't on the table. It was accepted each of us would take on one of the designated royal roles. So it was best not to consider anything else.' He looked at her. 'But do not feel sorry for me. I love my job; it gave me an opportunity to meet many people and I hope to do good, for Aguilarez and other countries too.' The trips abroad, to ravaged, war-torn countries, the children who had literally nothing, invaded his mind, the images stark and vivid. In truth, those were the people he wanted to help the most.

But when he had asked his parents if his role could change, become more humanitarian, if perhaps he could set up a foundation, take up a more hands-on role with charities close to his heart, they had vetoed the suggestion. Now when he could he made anonymous trips, made anonymous donations and wherever possible he used his diplomatic influence to increase foreign aid.

Seeing the way she scrutinised his expression, he pulled himself to the present. 'And as a diplomat I believe that it would be good for Aguilarez and Casavalle for us to marry.'

As the car started the steep, almost vertical climb up the mountain roads, she clutched her arm rest. 'Where does this lead?'

'To the palace of Aguilarez.'

'Oh.'

Her face scrunched with worry and he understood immediately. 'We aren't meeting my family or anything like that.' As the car slowed he nodded at her. 'Ready.'

'Hold on. I'll just put my toque on.' She smiled. 'It's a bit like a security blanket.'

He opened the door and climbed out at the gates that led to the Aguilarean royal palace. The gates were ornamental and spiky; set in the vast stone wall that surrounded the estate, they imposed their presence, made it clear that only those welcome could enter. Even now the temptation was there to look up and to check for defenders on the parapets.

Behind them a few hardy reporters had followed and cameras clicked and whirred. Reporters shouted questions. 'Are you taking the Princess to meet your family?'

This time Cesar stopped for a moment. 'Keep calm, guys. My family are not here. I am taking the Princess for a toboggan ride—on private royal property. No doubt we will see you again on our way out.'

A few photos later and they got back into the car and headed towards the palace.

'I hope tobogganing is acceptable?'

'Try and stop me. I love tobogganing. In fact, I, Princess of Casavalle, challenge you, the Prince of Aguilarez, to a race. Instead of fighting it out on the battlefield we'll take to the slopes.'

Her smile lit her face and he could almost feel it warm him. 'I accept the challenge, Princess. But, tell me, what is the winner's prize?' His gaze lingered on her expression, snagged on her lips. 'A kiss?'

A silence and then she tossed her head in a regal acceptance; he'd known she wouldn't back away from a challenge. 'Agreed.'

Gabi hadn't felt like this since she'd arrived in Casavalle—in truth she wasn't sure she'd felt like this ever. Her whole being felt alive as they stepped out of the car into the crisp sunlit air. 'It's beautiful,' she breathed. All around them was the brilliant white of the snow; the air tasted different at this altitude, tanged with cold and snow and dappled with sunlight. As she looked out at the peaks and crags and the loom of the palace in the distance she could feel exhilaration swell through her.

Turning, she faced him and now her heart pitter-pattered, leapt and bounded as she recalled their bet. Waited as he opened the boot of the car and tugged out two toboggans. Simple, sturdy and wooden, they looked brand new and Gabi had to admire Cesar's ability to make things happen.

'Right. This way,' he said, and they started to tramp across the snow to the start point at the top of a hill. 'A practice run and then we race?' he suggested and she nodded agreement and lowered herself on the toboggan.

And with that she was off, an adrenalin-fuelled cry left her lips and carried on the cold air as she zoomed over the compact white snow, manoeuvred the toboggan skilfully, oh, so aware of Cesar running parallel to her. The journey to the bottom of the hill was one of unalloyed joy and she climbed off and beamed at him. 'That was amazing. Now I'm ready to race.'

'Then let's do this.'

Once they were back at the top her breath caught and it was nothing to do with the uphill climb and everything to do with Cesar and his sheer masculine beauty, enhanced by the slight flush to his cheeks, the light in his brown eyes as they rested on her. 'May the best person win,' he stated.

This time the descent was different; oblivious to the scenery and driven by a desire to win, Gabi focused on the end goal. Balanced her weight, used her instincts and willed her toboggan to fly straight and true to the finish line ahead of Cesar. And in the final seconds she edged it, skimmed over the finish line by a whisker, climbed off the toboggan with a whoop of triumph. 'I did it.'

'You did.'

And as they stood there it was the most natural thing in the world for her to say, 'In which case, I claim the winner's prize.'

Stunned by her own daring...stupidity...madness, she stepped towards him; her hormones punched the air and did a happy dance. Her brain tried to intervene and Gabi shut it down. What better time, what better place than this? No fear of hidden cameras, of having this moment recorded and splashed across the media. And it wasn't as though she were committing to anything—it was just a kiss. The result of a challenge, no more.

Enough justification. She *wanted* to kiss him, wanted it with an intensity she had never experienced before.

Desire pulsed through her, seemed to make her veins fizz, propelled her forward so she was standing flush against him, so close she could smell his unique scent, and slowly she lifted a hand and placed it on his chest, on the thick cable-knit wool of his sweater.

Slowly, as if they had all the time in the world, his dark brown eyes fixed on hers, as if she were the only woman in the universe, and she wondered if it was possible to drown in anticipation. Her skin heated, her nerves end tingled and, wow, he hadn't even kissed her yet.

Then his lips touched hers, his fingers tangled in her hair and she was lost. The kiss was gentle, his lips firm against hers. She pressed against his body, his muscles hard, and he deepened the kiss, gave a small groan and her head whirled as she lost herself in the moment.

Time stood still and Gabi had no idea if the kiss lasted a minute or hours…but then a cold breeze gusted and penetrated the fog of desire and he broke the kiss. Gabi opened eyes she hadn't realised she'd closed and stared at him.

So much for just a kiss, nothing more. But she mustn't show how affected she was; she had to remember that for Cesar this was 'normal', that he'd shared millions of similar kisses with other women, more beautiful and sophisticated than Gabi could ever hope to be.

Play it cool.

'Thank you,' she said. 'That was a prize worth winning. Now how about a rematch but this time no prizes?'

'Sure.' There was something elusive in his voice but his expression maintained his usual easy charm. 'Let's get back to the top and when you're ready I've arranged for lunch in my quarters in the palace.'

* * *

An hour later Gabi followed Cesar through a side entrance and into the Aguilarean palace, caught a glimpse of her reflection in an enormous black gilded mirror and gave a small gasp of horror.

'You're sure no one will see me?'

'I'm sure. This is my private entrance.'

'Thank goodness. If Maria saw me now she'd…well, I'm not sure what she'd do but she wouldn't be happy.'

'Well, Maria isn't here and personally I think you look beautiful. I like the windswept look.'

'Wind-battered more like.' As they entered his apartment she glanced round. 'Is this where you lived before you left on diplomatic duties?'

'Yes.' His glance around was perfunctory. The room was comfortable without being ostentatious, the furniture sleek but comfortable. The flat-screen TV mounted on the wall was state of the art. Gabi liked it, she realised.

'Lunch should be here any minute.'

'In which case I will hide in the bathroom until it is,' Gabi stated firmly, suiting action to word.

Five minutes later she heard Cesar's, 'All clear,' and she exited. 'That looks delicious.' The table had been set beautifully with a centrepiece of flowers, silver cutlery and starched napkins.

'I think the kitchen staff want to impress you,' Cesar said.

'Consider me impressed.' Gabi grimaced. 'I should have come out and thanked whoever brought it. I didn't think.'

'It's OK. Daniella didn't realise you were hiding.'

'She just thought I was in the washroom—Maria

would say that's worse. I'm not sure royalty are supposed to use washrooms.'

She sat down opposite him. 'This is incredible.' A tantalising aroma of tangy lemon and thyme wafted up from her plate, where a portion of risotto was perfectly presented. In the centre of the table was a simple green salad. Gabi served herself and took a mouthful and closed her eyes in astonishment. 'The dressing is sublime.'

'I'm glad you like it.'

'I love it. I wish I could cook like this.' She took another mouthful and looked at him. 'Can you cook like this? I mean, does royalty get taught how to cook?'

'It is not part of the royal curriculum, no. There are royal chefs who prepare every meal.' He shrugged. 'I do remember wanting to learn how to bake but I couldn't convince anyone to show me how.'

'Your parents?'

Cesar gave a small laugh. 'My parents don't work like that. You met them, albeit briefly. Can you imagine either of them baking cookies? I very much doubt either of them has even entered the royal kitchens, unless it was for some sort of publicity shot.' He nodded. 'I think once my mother did pose with Flavia and me with a bowl and a wooden spoon. In fact, I think that's what triggered my desire to bake. The hope she'd actually make good.'

The words were matter-of-fact, said with a suggestion of lightness, but Gabi sensed an undercurrent of sadness, and an image of a young Cesar flashed across her brain. A small dark-haired boy who had *truly* hoped his mother would make good, make the publicity illusion into truth.

'Wasn't there anyone else? I mean, how does a royal childhood work?'

'There were many nannies.' Again there was a shadow in his eyes. 'And a royal agenda devised by our parents. An agenda that did not include baking. The idea being we had more important things to do, and achieve. That it was our privilege and our duty to act for Aguilarez and the ability to bake a cake would hardly advance our country in any way.'

'But that doesn't sound like much...fun.'

'Fun wasn't a priority in our childhood.'

Gabi wondered if that was how her father had thought, understood more now why her mother had panicked, hadn't wanted to bring her child up in the royal household, bound by royal rules.

'Is that what you believe? How you would want to bring up your children? Because that isn't my plan. I am going to be a hands-on parent and if my child wants to bake then my child will bake. And I don't care if it advances Casavalle or not.'

'I take it you know how to bake?'

'I do. My Aunt Bea taught me, though she didn't let me lick the spoon and it was what she called "functional baking". So that I would be able to make the meals, make useful things.' After Bea's death Gabi had discovered a well-thumbed book on how to raise a child, including a section on functional baking. The find had touched her, made her realise anew that Bea and Peter had been thrown into a guardianship they had been truly bewildered by. 'I always used to imagine, though, that my mother would have baked gooey chocolate creations with me, with sprinkles and icing and...' Sometimes the image had been so clear she had almost been able to hear Sophia's laughter. 'Not that I am complaining. Functional baking is important too.'

'It would be OK to complain.' Cesar hesitated. 'It must have been hard to lose your mother so young, however good your aunt and uncle were.'

'I don't really remember her, just a few elusive memories that I'm not even sure are true. And there are no photographs. I understand why now—she must have been worried about being recognised.'

'And you had no idea who your father was.'

'None. I know now that my aunt and uncle must have known—they can hardly have missed the fact that my mom married a king—but they maintained complete silence. All they told me was that my mother had never told them the identity of my father.' They had rarely spoken of Sophia and, soon realising they didn't like to discuss her mother, Gabi had stopped asking. Now she understood their reticence—the letter from her mother had explained that she had asked for the promise of secrecy, and Bea and Peter had maintained that promise to the end.

'That must have been hard.'

Gabi nodded. 'It was. In the end I made up a story; well, actually, I made up lots of stories. My father figured as a doctor, a soldier, a firefighter... Every hero in every book. Then every villain—I had him down as a criminal, a married man, et cetera, et cetera. Eventually I settled on a guy who couldn't deal with the idea of parenthood.' She lifted a hand to her face. 'The worst thing was wondering if I'd passed him on the street, or if he was a customer in the shop. The realisation I wouldn't have known him from Adam.'

Cesar studied her. 'I think you would have. If Vincenzo had met you—there is a definite family resemblance.'

'Did you know him well?'

'No, not really. I met him on formal occasions—he was a formal man. I am not sure if anyone knew him well. Perhaps your mother did, perhaps Maria did, but he wasn't a man who welcomed or wished for closeness. But he was a good ruler—he and Maria were respected and liked throughout Casavalle.'

The words were a reminder of why they were sitting here, to consider the idea of a marriage. One that would be like Vincenzo and Maria's—an alliance made in the hope of winning their people's respect and liking. A marriage that offered respect and liking but not love. Though she believed that Maria and Vincenzo had achieved a closeness and a mutually supportive marriage.

But she must be careful not to forget the boundaries, not get lost in the illusion.

Putting her cutlery down, she gestured to the table. 'That was delicious. Thank you, and thank you for the replacement history lesson. I truly enjoyed it.'

He glanced at his watch. 'But now you need to return to Casavalle. Of course. But you are happy to arrange another date? I believe we should attend Antonio and Tia's wedding together in three days' time, but if we can fit another date in before that we should.'

'Yes. But if it is OK with you, I'll arrange it.' It was time she took some sort of control; before he dazzled her into seeing this proposed marriage in a soft rose-tinted light. 'I'll contact you with the details.'

CHAPTER SEVEN

CESAR APPROACHED THE Casavallian palace, aware of a sense of well-being, a swell of happy expectation. He frowned, suddenly uneasy though he wasn't sure why. Campaign Marriage was going better than he could have hoped; the more he got to know Gabriella, the more he liked her, the more he believed that they could make a go of it. So there was no need for unease.

Instead he needed to continue the good work. He entered the palace, where a staff member greeted him and led him up the ornate winding stairs.

'Princess Gabriella is through here.' Cesar followed through a state guest apartment, through the richly furnished living area to a spacious kitchen, where Gabriella stood by the marble-topped counter.

She smiled at the retainer and thanked him and once the grey-haired man had left she turned to Cesar, who surveyed the preparations for their date. Two aprons, a recipe book and an array of ingredients, including a big mixing bowl and two wooden spoons.

'We're going to bake,' she explained. 'It's what you wanted to do when you were little and I thought it would be fun.'

Hell, there was that warmth again; the odd sensation of…of what? Being cared for?

'Don't worry,' she added. 'I have also alerted the press, who will be allowed to come in and take photos of us in our aprons and take a picture of the fruit of our labours.'

'What are we making?'

'Decadent chocolate cake.'

'Sounds good.'

'Yes. I haven't made it before. Imogen gave me the recipe book, said she'd heard it's good. I've got the ingredients, now I need to read the instruct…' Her voice trailed off and as he looked at her, he saw a small flush mount her cheeks.

'What's wrong?'

'Nothing,' she said quickly but she shielded the book with an arm as she spoke.

'Come on, Gabi. Tell me.'

'There's nothing to tell… It's…well…the instructions… they are a little…um…racy.'

He raised his eyebrows. 'Racy?'

'Look. It really doesn't matter. It just implies the cake has some…well…aphrodisiac properties.'

'I think I'd like to see this.'

'No…really.' Quickly she shut the book and moved it out of his reach as he headed closer to her. Grabbed it as he reached for it and turned to face him with a shake of her head, her back against the counter, holding it above her head, with a half-laugh.

'Nowhere to go,' he said teasingly.

And then he realised how close she was, so very tantalisingly close; he could smell the scent of pine from the tree mixed with her clean vanilla-spiced scent, and desire spun his head. As if she felt the exact same thing, her hand dropped to her side, still holding the damned book.

'I don't think we need any help from the cake,' he murmured. And then he was kissing her, kissing her as if his life depended on it and it felt…incredible. Magnificent.

He heard the thud as the book fell to the kitchen floor and she moved against him, and he entangled his hands in her hair, the soft silken tresses against his fingers, deepened the kiss and tasted her gasp of pleasure. Then all that existed was the scale of his desire; he wanted this woman with an unparalleled fierceness and it was only the recognition of the depth of that yearning that penetrated the fog of desire. Reminded him who this woman was. Gabriella Ross Valenti, soon to be Queen of Casavalle. This had to stop here, before he was no longer able to stop.

He gently disengaged, his breathing laboured. Each jagged breath seemed to accelerate his heartbeat further—just looking at her flushed face, the desire-dazed look in her eyes—and he wanted to kiss her again and hang the consequences.

OK. Stop right there.

For once he couldn't think of what to say.

'I…' She stopped, reached out a hand to the counter as if to steady herself and tried again. 'I…we can't keep doing this—kissing on every date.' Her voice still hitched. 'It's… I'm worried it will mess with my head, fuzz my judgement and I…we can't afford that. The decision we have to make is too important for that.'

'Agreed. If you decide to marry me I need to know it is for the right reasons; I need to know we entered this agreement on the same page.'

She smoothed her hair, ran a wondering hand over her lips and nodded.

Forcing positivity into his voice, he gestured to the ingredients. 'Now let's bake this cake.'

A nod and she leant down, picked the book up off the floor with a rueful look, and found the page with the recipe.

The first ten minutes were spent in sharing the tasks, whilst fighting off the memory of that kiss. No easy task in itself, as they were of necessity still so close that he could catch a waft of her shampoo. As he read the instructions over her shoulder he had to fight the urge to lean over and nuzzle kisses along the nape of her neck. Knew the smell of cocoa powder as it dusted the air would always bring him back to this moment.

'It's good practice for children, isn't it?' she said and he blinked.

'I think I may have missed a bit of the conversation.'

'I meant that one day I can imagine showing my child how to do this and it got me wondering.' She turned her face from him, stirred the mixture in the bowl harder and then paused, turned to look at him. 'Tell me what sort of father you want to be.'

'Why do I get the feeling this is an interview question?'

'Because in a way it is.' Her voice was serious now. 'If we get married it's not like a fairy tale where we waltz off the page into the horizon of happy ever after. We have to think about the reality of what comes after we say we do. This is real.'

'I understand that,' he said.

'Good.' She stirred with a little less gusto and then handed it over to him to continue. Almost as if it were some sort of symbol. 'So what sort of father *do* you want to be? You must have thought about this, thought about the idea of having children?'

'Um...' He stared down at the mixture in the bowl, searched for inspiration. In truth the furthest he'd got to thinking about children was the general idea of not having them.

Because the whole idea of parenthood terrified him. When he remembered how much he'd craved affection, love, attention, he knew that that was what he needed to give a child. Problem was he wasn't sure he could, because he'd never been shown how, and the thought of letting a child down was unacceptable. If there was any chance of that he wouldn't take the risk. An easy choice as he'd had no intention of marriage anyway.

But now... That had all changed and panic clawed his chest. How on earth could he be a father? The idea threatened to choke him with its enormity. What if he really couldn't be the father he knew every child deserved, couldn't offer love? What if he was simply conditioned to repeat his parents' mistakes?

Gabriella was studying him. 'Sorry. I know it's a big question. But it is an important one. If we are to get married then hopefully we will end up responsible for another human being and that is an awesome and a huge responsibility. And here and now I am willing to put my credentials on the line. I have always wanted children, but only if it would be right for them. I wanted it to be the right time in my life so that I would be able to give them security, a home, as well as love. I wanted them to have a family life with two loving parents and siblings and huge Christmas meals and family holidays and...' She shook her head. 'I know I am painting a rose-coloured picture. I know there will be difficulties and arguments and tiredness along the way. I do know it will be real. But I want all that too.'

A family. Kids in the plural. Christmas lunches. Family holidays. Events completely unlike the ones he'd experienced. Himself and Gabriella with a brood of dark-haired children, children with Gabriella's wide smile and dimple. With her serious brown eyes, that could light up with laughter. The wave of panic threatened again and he forced himself to stem it as he faced the seriousness of her expression now.

As she continued. 'I didn't have a father and I wanted one so very badly. I vowed that when I had children I would make sure I gave them a good dad, a good man who would care for them, protect them, carry them round on his shoulders, help them with their homework…be there for them. I can't marry a man who won't be a good father.'

'I…' Dammit—she deserved better than the platitudes he knew he could reel out, the diplomatic assurances he could craft. 'I'll do my best,' he said, the lameness apparent to his own ears, and he knew she deserved more than that as well. He watched as she carefully spooned the mixture into a cake tin. 'I realise that sounds meh at best. But it's hard for me to imagine being a good father, because I don't have a role model. And I don't have the sort of imagination you have to be able to picture one.'

'What about your own father?'

Cesar hesitated and then shrugged, knew she deserved a real explanation. 'My parents…they did everything for duty, for Aguilarez. Including having children; sometimes I felt as though we were their gift to the country, a duty done. Then after we were born it was their duty to mould us into the sons and daughters of Aguilarez. But by so doing it was as if that absolved them of any duty to make us feel wanted on a personal level. So I saw very little of him and when I did it was more of an audience, an update report, a tick-the-box exercise.' He could still remember the discomfort of the starched clothes, the perfectly combed hair, the exhortations from the nanny of the day not to fidget, to enunciate, to be polite. 'A time where I had to be on best behaviour.'

'And did you always behave?'

'Yes. Especially once I'd figured out that it wasn't only us who bore the consequences if I didn't, but it was the nannies too.' He flushed now, slightly uncomfortable. 'It sounds horrible now but I did realise that gave me a level of power. It was always easier to persuade them to give us a treat just before a parental meeting.'

Gabriella looked at him. 'So your childhood was really a string of negotiations.'

'Life is a string of negotiations,' he said.

'Maybe, but it shouldn't be and childhood certainly shouldn't be that. And I don't want it to be that way for my children.'

'Neither do I.' And that was the honest truth. 'I would do my best, Gabi. To be there for them, to kick a ball around, teach them how to ride a bike or bake a cake. I'll try to be there for them.' Somehow he'd conquer the terror that twisted his guts with the fear he'd get it wrong. After all, Cesar Asturias feared nothing.

'Thank you,' she said softly. 'Sometimes all we can do is our best.'

And he was man who had always made sure his best was good enough.

Picking up the cake tin, he went over and popped it

into the oven. 'As this has become a kind of interview, I too have a question I need to ask. Perhaps we could have coffee whilst the cake bakes and we can talk.'

Gabi's head whirled as it tried to process the information he had given her about royal childhoods. Cold, damaging, miserable, sad…all those words chased each other around her head. Most of all though she wanted to offer comfort, but she knew that would not be welcomed.

'Fire away,' she said as the smell of the cake, the rich deep chocolate, started to pervade the kitchen.

He waited until he had made the coffee and she accepted the cup with appreciation.

'There is something we have not spoken of,' he said. 'My relationships have been in the public domain, but we have never discussed your past relationships.' He raised a hand. 'I am not trying to pry but from a publicity angle I do need to know if any ex-suitors will come out of the woodwork.'

Gabriella shook her head. 'I had two relationships. Both serious at the time.' Though now, somehow the memories had faded, seemed blurred and sepia.

'Tell me.' The words were a touch on the curt side and for one dizzying, stupid moment Gabriella wondered if it bothered him. Then her brain told her not to be stupid. As if. Cesar didn't care. Any more than she cared about all his exes.

Only that wasn't true, was it? She did care, not because she was jealous, but because they made her feel inadequate. For an instant an image of his most recent girlfriend, Lady Amelia Scott-Browne, popped into her head even though she knew that Lady Amelia and Cesar had broken up some time ago. Yet Lady Amelia had been so poised, beautiful, always immaculate, elegant, versed in which knife and fork to use.

Realising that he was still waiting, she regrouped. 'Steve and Paul.' Resolutely she pulled them to mind. Steve—blond, blue-eyed, medium build, kind features, slightly receding hairline, sweet, average. Paul, brown-haired, hazel-eyed, craggy features, long hair, sweet, average. 'They were both really nice guys. But somehow it didn't pan out either time. I met Steve very soon after my aunt and uncle passed away and I was in the throes of grief and I dealt with that by throwing myself into work. I got so caught up in the book store that in the end he got frustrated. Wanted a girlfriend who had more time for him. I was sad. But I understood.'

Cesar frowned. 'Surely he could have been supportive, understood how important it was to you.'

'Perhaps,' Gabriella said. 'But I was…well, I was quite obsessed really and I should have been more willing to spend more time with him. It was the same with Paul. He wanted me to slow down. We both wanted the same things; we just had different ideas about how it would work. He assumed when we got married, I'd sell up or delegate more and I didn't want to do that. Or at least it never quite seemed the right time. In the end they both moved on.'

'But you loved them both.'

Gabriella looked back into the past. Had she loved them? 'I genuinely believed we matched; were on the same page, could bring up children together and have a normal, happy family life.' The thing she'd craved all her life. 'But in the end I wasn't enough for them.'

So how on earth could she ever be enough for this man? Doubts swirled. She'd been with Steve and Paul for eighteen months and two years respectively. That was the length of time she could keep an average man—what hope did she have with Cesar?

It was a relief when the ping of the oven indicated the cake was ready.

CHAPTER EIGHT

TWO DAYS LATER Cesar gave his reflection a perfunctory check, made sure there was no spot on his tie, no dust on his suit because, despite the fact that Antonio and Tia's wedding was to be private, there would still be photographers covering the arrival and departure of guests—a fact he had every intention of using to his advantage.

His and Gabriella's.

He rolled his eyes as he caught the small goofy smile on his lips, brought about by the thought of Casavalle's Queen-in-waiting.

Enough. There was no need for goofiness, rather the smile should be one of satisfaction, that his courtship was going well, that there was a certainty of a union less cold than that of his parents. The kisses they had shared had shown him that—his body still tied in knots.

Turning away from his reflection, he headed for the door and the chauffeur-driven car that would take him to Casavalle, where he'd arranged to meet Gabriella prior to the ceremony, so they could make the walk to the chapel together.

Forty-five minutes later he alighted in the courtyard, raised a hand in acknowledgement as the photographers clicked, made sure that the small package was just visible in the pocket of his suit as he entered the palace and made his way to the reception room.

He pushed open the door, and felt his lungs constrict slightly. The dress she wore was perfect for the occasion, navy blue, simple in its structural cut and demure neckline, but made that little bit different by the statement flared sleeves. Her chestnut hair fell free to her shoulders. 'You look stunning,' he said simply.

Gabriella looked down at herself. 'I have to admit I am having doubts. Fashion was never my thing.'

'It's beautiful,' he assured her.

'You've scrubbed up pretty well yourself.'

'Apart from the shadows under my eyes,' he said, with a smile. 'I stayed up late reading.'

'You did?'

'I did.' In truth it had started as a homework exercise— he wanted to be able to show Gabriella that he had tried. Had decided to read a chapter. But to his astonishment the book had gripped him, and it had only been the chime of the clock at an advanced hour that had forced him to turn the light out. 'It was a good choice.'

'I'm glad.'

'Now *I* have brought you this.' He handed her a slim box, watched as she opened it to reveal a posy of flowers designed so that they could be pinned to her dress.

'From the Aguilarean palace gardens.'

Her brown eyes surveyed him. 'So if I wear it, it will send out a subtle romantic message for the press to pick up on. And it could also be seen as a symbol of our countries' friendship.'

'Yes.'

'An excellent prop,' she said coolly. 'For our double act.'

'That is what I thought. I also hoped you would like

them; I did pick them myself.' He hesitated. 'Is something wrong?'

Her expression relaxed. 'Yes…no… It's just hard for me to get my head round a political alliance and fake romance. Our last two "dates" were different, more private—the press were hardly there. Today they will be watching and I don't want them to focus on us rather than on Antonio and Tia's wedding and—'

'Hey. Slow down. There would be public interest in you regardless of our supposed romance. And from what I know of Antonio he will be more than happy for the attention to be diverted from him.'

She inhaled a deep breath and he watched her straighten up. 'You're right.'

'I am. Now let me pin it on,' he said, seeing her small grimace of frustration as she made the attempt.

He headed towards her, aware that he was holding his breath as he carefully pinned the arrangement to her dress, closed his eyes briefly at her proximity, at the sheen of her chestnut hair, the scent of jasmine that tantalised his senses. Felt the tiny shudder that rippled her body and knew she felt it too.

'Shall we go?' Her voice was breathless as she stepped back. 'I said we would meet everyone else in the reception hall, then we can all walk to the chapel together. Antonio is already at the church with Luca. But the rest of the party is here.'

He nodded. 'Tia, her mother Grace, Miles.' The palace secretary who, rumour had it, had fallen hard for Tia's mother, Grace Phillips.

'Yes. Antonio has also invited Gina and Enrico, who are valued staff members, and Tia has asked her bosses from the UK—Lucia and Giovanni. They are lovely.' She glanced at him. 'No doubt you've done your research.'

'Of course. I am here, after all, to represent Aguilarez.' He smiled at her. 'But after the wedding I have our next "date" planned.' And again there was the sense of anticipation. 'We are going on a plane journey so I can show you an aerial view of our countries.'

'Another geographical history lesson?'

'Perhaps. But it is also a venue where the press cannot follow us—where we can be private. So if you are worried about the press now just think about later, when we will escape them.'

'Thank you.' Her smile was genuine and he felt a satisfaction at being responsible for the lightening of tension in her face.

They walked down the marbled hall, then entered the reception room. He smiled at Tia, whom he had briefly met at the presentation ball. She was pretty and right now she glowed with a radiance it was impossible to ignore. She was dressed in a simple floaty, flowered dress, her happiness evident, as was her pride in her pregnancy, shown by the protective hand over the curve of her belly. They were doing the right thing, but again the timing of this could not be worse. More scandal, more rumour and speculation.

But now wasn't the time for this. Now was the time to focus on the small talk, circulate the group, chat to each and every one. Then the walk across the courtyard to the chapel; this was all important as he knew there would be eagle-eyed reporters who would spot the flowers pinned to Gabriella's dress, would also note how close they stood together. Zoom in on the light touch to her arm as he pointed something out. Satisfaction at a job well done inexplicably battled with a frisson of un-ease, the knowledge that he took way more than a clini-cal pleasure in her closeness. A strange desire to protect her, mixed with more primeval desire.

It was with relief that he entered the chapel, heard Gabi's intake of breath, and as he looked round he un-derstood why.

'It's spectacular,' she breathed as Tia turned to her mum.

'Mum. It's gorgeous, perfect. Thank you.'

The older woman beamed and suddenly Cesar felt a small wrench—his own mother had never once looked at him like that; no one had. Next to him he felt Gabi tense, knew she was missing her own mother.

'You're welcome, sweetheart. It wasn't just me, though. I couldn't have done it without Miles.'

Next to her the palace secretary smiled self-deprecatingly, but his expression as he stepped closer to Grace Phillips was full of warmth and affection.

'I know that and I truly appreciate all your help, Miles. With everything.'

Tia's mum suffered from chronic fatigue and there-fore her words were not mere gloss, they were valid. And that made Miles' love even more worthy. In sickness and in health. Words Cesar planned to say soon enough to the woman standing next to him now. And again the thought made the whole plan more real, more intimate, made moisture sheen his neck.

As he followed Gabriella to the front pew to join Imo-gen and Queen Maria he glanced to the front where An-tonio stood, upright and proud, his entire being focused on his bride. It was not Antonio Valenti's way to show emotion, but the look in his eyes said it all for him. And again Cesar wanted to shift from foot to foot, felt inexplicably small and uncomfortable as the ceremony progressed.

Grace walked her daughter down the aisle and it was impossible now to believe this marriage was one simply of honour, when he saw the way Antonio and Tia looked at each other, the way they exchanged their vows as if each and every word mattered, love abounded in every syllable. He glanced over at Luca and Imogen and saw how they looked at each other, the way they held hands. Then of course there was Tia's mother and the palace secretary. Everywhere he looked there was an aura of love and it was making him distinctly uncomfortable, especially when he thought he detected a hint of wistfulness in Gabriella's smile.

For a moment he wondered if he should have swallowed his scruples and pretended to offer her love, pretended to emulate the sap and pap and sighs and giddiness. But how could that work? How could he build this union on illusion and deceit? How would he be able to sustain the illusion for decades? And he had no wish for or ability to feel real love. After all, if you'd never been shown love how could you feel it? And why give anyone that sort of power over you anyway? So better for them both to go into marriage with the same goals. That was the way to build a working relationship, a lasting partnership.

He returned his focus to the couple at the front. 'You may kiss the bride.'

Antonio leaned forward and, oh, so gently...oh, so filled with awe, as if Tia was the most precious person on this earth, he kissed her.

Around him Cesar could hear the intake of breath,

had no doubt there was a tear in the corner of every eye except his as the swell of classical music touched the air.

The now wed couple walked back down the aisle, their faces lit up, hand in hand, and soon the small congregation followed. 'That was beautiful,' Gabriella said and now he could hear the wistfulness in her voice, knew she didn't mean the actual quality of the dress or the flowers. She meant the love that permeated the occasion. And that he couldn't offer her.

Gabi admired the beautifully decorated room, one of the numerous reception rooms in Casavalle's palace. Once again she marvelled at the décor, given how busy everyone had also been with Christmas preparations.

But it was more than that; Grace Phillips had wanted to make this beautiful and personal for her daughter. And she had definitely succeeded. She must have spent a long time considering how to make this room different from the others and she'd done so through simplicity. The whole room was themed with green and white, the use of delicate white flowers and green foliage almost ethereally pretty. Delicate, fresh, new and somehow joyous.

Gabi looked round at the small gathering of people and swallowed the lump in her throat. Just months ago she hadn't known these people, even that this place existed. Now she had a family. Two brothers, now a sister-in-law and soon she would be an aunt.

Her gaze skimmed to Cesar, who was chatting to Antonio, looking relaxed and smiling. This was a man who wanted her to be a wife, a mother to their children. The idea was so surreal she closed her eyes. Images hit her—of a small dark-haired boy with Cesar's brown eyes.

'You OK?'

She turned to see Imogen, her best friend, now also her brother's fiancée, at her side. 'I'm fine. Are you OK?' She saw Imogen's eyes rest on Tia, one hand on her belly.

'Yes. I am happy for Tia. Truly I am. As for us, Luca says we will figure out a way to have a family if that's what we want. But if it doesn't work out I am more than enough for him.' Imogen's lips curved up into a smile. 'And the wonderful thing is I know he is telling the truth, because I feel the same way.'

There was a twinge of envy again, but alongside it was the knowledge that it would be easier, less pressured for Luca and Imogen now that he wouldn't be ruler. Did Cesar have a point—maybe love was more 'affordable', more likely to thrive if you weren't a ruler.

Imogen's gaze turned to Cesar and then turned back to Gabi. 'Tell me, what is going on there? I saw the speculations in the press, but I've learnt to take them with a hefty pinch of salt.'

'It's complicated.' Gabi could feel her skin heat and her gaze skittered away from Imogen's blue eyes. 'We're just spending some time together.'

Imogen raised her eyebrows. 'So there is some truth to the press reports.'

'No...yes... It's...complicated.'

'Isn't it always with these royal princes?' Imogen grinned and somehow Gabi felt more grounded. After all, Imogen's life had completely changed as well and she had never seen her friend happier. Ah. But Imogen was in love, had a fiancé who adored her. Love was not on the table here and this marriage was a negotiation, each date the equivalent of a meeting shrouded in the illusion of romance.

Before she could say any more Luca and Cesar headed

over to them as Antonio tapped a spoon against his glass and once the hum of conversation subsided, he began to speak.

'As you all know, we decided to keep this ceremony private as both Tia and I wanted something simple with just friends and family. We also decided to forgo the usual formal speeches, but I would like to briefly say how very, very happy I am. Tia means the world to me and I cannot wait to welcome our baby into the world. My only regret is that my father is not here and neither is Tia's brother, Nathan, my best friend, who died in the line of duty. I would have been honoured to have him as my best man.' He raised a glass. 'To those we've lost.'

Gabi lifted her glass, felt the ache of grief for the father she'd never known, the mother she barely remembered except as an elusive voice, a scent, a feeling of arms around her. For her aunt and uncle who had taken her in for duty but had at least not abandoned her, had provided her with a roof, with food and a muted love. For Tia's brother, Nathan, taken at the prime of life. Like Sophia, a life cut tragically short.

Next to her she felt Cesar move closer to her, took comfort from his warmth.

Now Tia stepped forward.

'I miss Nathan more than I can say. But I know exactly what he'd say now. He'd want us to get on and celebrate—appreciate what we have and enjoy the moment. He would be thrilled his best friend was marrying his little sister—and I hope and believe that somehow, somewhere he does know and is giving us his blessing. I would also like to raise my glass now to my mother, who is the most loving, wonderful mother a daughter could ever hope for.'

Once more glasses were raised and soon after that waiters circulated with more canapés; soft music played in the background until it came time for the newly-weds to leave.

Gabi moved forward to hug them. 'I am so happy for you both,' she said.

'Thank you, big sister.'

'It still feels strange to hear you say that.'

'But it is true.' Antonio spoke softly now. 'Gabi. Follow your heart—and do not let anyone pressure you into anything simply to win approval. Things have changed in the Valenti family—duty is important but not at the cost of your happiness.'

Gabi looked at him, wondered if he knew of or suspected Cesar's plans. Perhaps to a royal they were obvious.

'Thank you, and have a wonderful honeymoon.'

Once the happy couple had been waved off Cesar turned to Gabi. 'Shall we go?'

Gabi glanced at him, sure that the man next to her, despite the smile on his lips and all the suave sophistication on show, wanted to shake the dust off his feet and flee the wedding and the company.

'I'll change into something more comfortable and then, yes, I'm ready.'

An hour later Cesar felt a loosening of tension as the Cessna levelled out flying over the verdant ever green beauty of Casavalle. It felt good to be flying high above the cloying confetti-strewn scenes of everlasting love, good to watch Gabriella's expression as she gazed out at the panoramic vista. He wanted to see her smile; knew that the wedding of her brother had brought mixed emotions for her as well as for him. The clusters of deep green trees that dotted the sweep and roll of the snow-dusted hills, the misty, mystical crags and peaks of Aguilarez's mountainous terrain in the distance were more than enough to bring a sense of joy.

For a while they gazed out in a silence only broken by the thrum of the plane's engines. Then she turned to him. 'It's awe-inspiring. It gives you are a real perspective— up here I feel free. Up here if I wanted to I could take off my boots and wriggle my bare toes and no one would tell me I was breaching royal protocol. I could paint my nails bright scarlet.'

'If you'd told me I'd have brought some nail polish.'

Her smile was rueful. 'It's mad, really. I never wanted to paint them scarlet before—it's only now I know I can't.'

Her honesty made him smile in return. 'It will become easier; once your position is more settled, once you get used to all the rules. Then you'll be able to figure out which ones you can break. And you'll learn the all-important royal requirement—how to wear a mask. That helps.'

'Is that what you were doing today?'

The question caught him off guard. 'Meaning?'

'At the wedding I got the impression you were…not uncomfortable, exactly, but that there were other places you'd rather be.' Surprise creased his forehead; how on earth had Gabriella noticed that? Hell, he must be losing his royal diplomatic touch.

'I did find the whole event…a little disconcerting,' he admitted. 'It was hard to believe the evidence of my eyes—to see the Valenti princes behaving in a way that seems so out of character. I knew the court had changed since the King's death but I had not expected to see Antonio, usually so reserved, so outwardly happy. And Luca—he is like a different person with Imogen.'

'And you disapprove.'

'It is not my place to approve or disapprove. It just felt surreal.'

There was a silence. 'I think it took both my brothers by surprise as well. Neither of them intended to fall in love.' She inhaled an audible breath. 'So maybe it could happen to you.'

'No.' The word unequivocal, no quarter or doubt, because he needed her to know that if she married him, she must not harbour delusions of or hope for love. 'That will not happen to me.'

'I don't understand how you can be so sure. As you said yourself, both Luca and Antonio have changed their stance towards love.'

Cesar suspected that Luca and Antonio had been able to show love, feel love because their upbringing, though similarly rooted in duty, had also contained love. True, King Vincenzo had been distant, formal, but he had once known the headiness of love with Gabriella's mother, and had had a good relationship with Queen Maria, even though it had not been a love match. And Queen Maria was a little softer than his own mother, had managed to temper the dictates of duty with some show of feeling towards her children. Perhaps made them believe in the possibility of love, made them foolish enough to open up to the risks. 'But I'm not made that way.'

'So what if *you* too change your mind?' she asked. Then, as if reading his expression, she raised her hand, her face flushing, sheer horror in her eyes. 'Oh, God. I don't mean do you think you will fall in love with me! I meant what if you fall in love with someone else?' Cesar frowned; why would she assume it would be possible for him to fall in love but not with her? 'Like Meribel did.'

'That will not happen.' How to convince her of something he knew with bone-deep certainty? 'Love is not in my vocabulary, not in my dictionary, not in my lexicon. Look at the mess and misery Meribel caused. I know Luca says that she did no wrong, that there is nothing to forgive.' He had been there when Luca had met with his sister, had admired the Valenti prince's eloquence and generosity. 'I know he now believes love trumps duty, that love is a driving force, but, whilst I respect that belief, I am not made that way.'

And so whilst he would not have chosen marriage he had accepted the necessity, and now as he looked at Gabriella it no longer felt like a life sentence—instead it felt like something that could work.

'I truly believe a marriage will work better without love. If Meribel had not met Dana, not fallen pregnant, if the marriage had gone through as planned, then Luca and she could have, would have been happy together.'

'But not as happy as they are now?'

Cesar shrugged, looked out of the window over the vast vista, where green and grey and brown swathed the landscape, the people not even tiny dots. 'Who knows? Love brings its own risks, of loss and grief. It complicates life. If we marry you do not need to fear I will fall in love with anyone.' He could hear the twist of disdain in his voice, hastened to sweeten it. 'I will be a one-woman man. Your man.'

Now awareness shimmered on the air, in echo of the mist outside, and the words felt like a vow. 'I would not be unfaithful—in truth I cannot imagine why I would want to be.'

As he looked at her, saw her gaze out over a country

she had been called upon to rule, he was struck anew by her beauty, and by a visceral desire. Her brown eyes held vulnerability and doubt. 'How can you know that? You are a man who is used to variety—you've been with so many beautiful women. How can you possibly swap from a playboy lifestyle to that of a married man?'

It was a fair question. 'It will not be a problem.'

'They are easy words to say.' She turned to him. 'After all, just a couple of months ago you were involved, had a girlfriend. Amelia. Amelia Scott-Browne.' A ghost of a smile. 'That is common knowledge. She is blonde and beautiful and titled. Yet you've got over her remarkably quickly.'

'I was involved with Amelia but not in any deep sense. We had an agreeable interlude but it was never serious. There was nothing to get over.'

On his part, anyway; yet he had for once completely miscalculated with Amelia and annoyance tugged his gut as their break-up scene flashed into his mind.

'Amelia, we have had a good time, have we not? A lot of fun. But this is a good time for an ending. I must go back to my country and help sort out the problems there.'

'I can wait.'

It was then he'd realised it was going to be difficult.

'Perhaps now is a good time to talk about beginnings, not endings. I want to marry you, Cesar. I love you and I believe you love me.'

Yet her green eyes had held assessment rather than love, or was that wishful thought on his part?

'I would make an excellent ambassadorial wife. No scandal, always the right conversation, and I'm good with people. We could make it work.'

As he'd listened, his brain had whirred. There would

be time for anger at himself later; now he had to figure out damage limitation.

'I am sorry, Amelia, but I will not marry you. There is no question of love. You always knew that.'

'But I thought that when you saw how well I understood your needs you would change your mind. Think of all I can offer you, Cesar.'

'I have no doubt you would make an excellent ambassadorial wife, Amelia. But you know full well that I never had any intention or desire to get married. And if I do it will only be for my country's benefit. That is as it is. But I would like us to part amicably.'

Her green eyes had narrowed in what now seemed obvious calculation. *'It wouldn't be a good time for another scandal to hit your country.'*

So much for love, he thought.

'It wouldn't,' he'd agreed easily. *'But in the long term it would hurt you more than it would me. I still won't marry you, and neither will anyone else in diplomatic circles.'*

Her eyes had widened and her lips had tipped up into a smile that hadn't reached them.

'I understand that, and of course I wouldn't cause a scandal.' Her voice had emerged through gritted teeth. *'I hope that we can remain friends.'*

Thus they had parted, and in truth he had given Amelia very little thought since, his focus on the events here and his impending marriage. And in the past days on Gabriella, who was looking at him with a troubled expression.

'So you could walk away without a regret, just move on?'

'Yes.' There was little point in pretence. 'I have always

been upfront with any woman I have been involved with that I could not offer permanence or anything serious.'

'But what if it had become deeper? What if you had started to have feelings for each other?'

'I don't know,' he said simply. 'But that never did happen.' He'd made sure it couldn't, kept it all light and on a superficial level. 'I always made sure that I kept the relationships short term. Prevention is better than cure, after all.'

'You make it sound like an illness, a disease that you have had to avoid.'

'Not an illness but a foolishness that I have been happy to avoid.' Why risk hurt or being hurt?

'All these women, Lady Amelia, the others, they meant nothing to you?' Now Gabriella looked horrified. 'They were *meaningless*. Yet you think you can sustain a marriage.'

Now irritation sparked in him. 'Those women weren't meaningless. They were all individuals who I liked, who liked me. We spent time together, enjoyable time, had fun. But a future together was never an end game; I made that clear at the outset and they were in complete agreement. With you the rules are different. A future together is the start point.'

'So you're offering me the long-term, marriage-included package deal.'

'Exactly. And I fully intend it to be a sustainable working partnership.' Cesar gave an inward wince. Could he make this any less appealing? Time to lighten it up. 'I also propose that we have some fun and, of course, there is also great sex on offer.'

The change of tactic caused a small gasp to fall from

her lips. 'You can't really expect me to marry you for great sex?'

'Not *just* for great sex. But it would be a bonus.' He wiggled his eyebrows. 'A big bonus.'

Gabriella gave a half-choke of laughter and shook her head. 'I cannot believe you said that.'

Cesar grinned and shrugged. 'Why not? In a negotiation it is important to stress the benefits on offer.' He met her gaze and now his tone was serious. 'I think it does matter. The attraction between us. It is a good thing.' This he knew—he'd seen how lack of passion led to a coldness, an aura of apathy and indifference. A stifled joyless atmosphere.

Gabi looked at him closely, studied his expression and he continued.

'I can offer you liking, respect, support, fidelity, fun, great sex.' He took a deep breath. 'But I can't offer you love. So our marriage won't work if love is what you want.' Cesar felt his jaw tense as he awaited her answer, knew it would essentially be the make or break in the negotiations. Hoped she could see that his offer was a better proposition than the uncertainties and vagaries of love. Watched as she turned away and looked out of the window. Realised he was holding his breath as he waited for her answer.

Gabi looked out over the jagged mountainous magnificence of Aguilarez. To her left the sweeping green of the Casavallian hills. Their countries were separated by a border and so much more, yet shared the same island, both surrounded by deep blue ocean. Sharing a history and two cultures, friendship and enmity that spanned centuries. There would have been alliances through marriage in the past; no doubt she wasn't the first ruler of Casavalle to weigh the necessity of love.

She'd always assumed she'd marry for love but now… the assumption blurred and faded. Liking, support, respect, fidelity, fun and, of course, the great sex. There was so much to be said for that. The idea of someone to help bear the weight and responsibility of ruling, a prince at her side who understood how it all worked. The fact that simply by saying I do she would help unite their two countries—surely the enormity of that outweighed the need for love.

A love she might never find anyway. Especially now. How would she ever know whether someone loved her for herself or for her position? Even if someone did fall for her how could she expect them to give up their life, their privacy and end up in the spotlight with her? If she fell in love with an 'ordinary' person what chance would that love have?

Imogen would say that love conquered all, that it would be possible to work it out. Whilst Cesar would say that that was a risk not worth the taking.

What would her parents have said? Gabi wondered. They had fallen in love, must have married with so much hope and happiness for the future.

Just eighteen months later her mother had fled, convinced that she was the wrong wife for a king, not wanting to bring her child up as a royal. Then, when she'd decided to give love a chance, it was too late. The King had met Maria and Sophia had decided not to complicate his life.

Had she been right or wrong? Gabi didn't know.

She remembered the words of Sophia's letter, every syllable etched on her brain.

Gabriella,

I want you to know that I did love your father, but I do believe he was better without me.

Love complicated his life. I complicated his life—I won't risk that again. Not now he has found a suitable wife who will, I hope, make him happy in a way I never could.

And Vincenzo had been happy; however much he had loved Sophia he hadn't tried to track her down, had granted the divorce without any attempt to persuade her to change her mind. Why? Luca believed it had been pride. But perhaps Vincenzo had known that love and ruling could not go hand in hand. Perhaps he had believed Sophia would be happier without him. She'd never know and that brought sadness with it; this decision was hers alone to make. But perhaps she could learn from the past. Maria and Vincenzo had been happy; they had done right by each other and Casavalle. Perhaps she needed to do the same.

Here above their two countries, where she could almost see the dividing line that separated them, she knew she had to do all in her power to serve her country, to keep the beautiful island below them united and at peace. But doubts still crowded in…this was still her life. Hers and his. And she wouldn't, couldn't rush into a decision here and now.

She turned to face Cesar. 'Love isn't a necessary component in any arrangement we may come to. I am not yet ready to make a final decision, so this isn't anywhere near a done deal, but I'm willing to go on to the next stage of negotiations.'

Relief touched his face as his shoulders relaxed and

then he smiled. 'That sounds good to me. I believe we can build a happy marriage, based on attraction, trust, shared beliefs and a desire to do the right thing for our countries. It is now my job to persuade you of that.'

His job. Negotiations. It was now his remit to bring negotiations to a close and suddenly a sheen of sadness touched her thoughts, an idea that this wasn't how it was supposed to be. But it was as it was. She wasn't Gabi Ross book-store owner any more—she was a princess, soon to be Queen, and she had to think differently.

'So we will continue to date,' Cesar continued, 'and I will continue to liaise with Miles over the publicity angles.'

Cesar and Miles did their job all too well, as it turned out. Because over the next few days, to Gabi's astonishment and discomfort, the media, expertly encouraged by Cesar and Miles, went nuts for the romance angle. A number of dates and occasions were agreed, and through necessity, given the number of royal engagements in her diary, Cesar simply came with her.

And... Gabi no longer knew how she felt. About anything. Could no longer distinguish between reality and illusion. All she did know was his proximity messed with her head and made the public engagements paradoxically both harder and easier.

Harder because she was on edge, her body preternaturally aware of him at all times, ever conscious that she had to act like a woman falling in love. Easier because with Cesar at her side she felt less alone; less daunted by the fear of making a mistake.

Thank goodness she and Imogen had decided to sneak

a little girl time this evening; as if on cue there was a knock on the door. 'Come in.'

Imogen entered and as always Gabi felt a rush of gratitude that she hadn't lost her friend, that Imogen had come with her on this royal journey.

Imogen smiled widely at her. 'Now, let's not waste time.' She sat down on the armchair in front of the fire, tucked her legs under her and accepted the glass of red wine Gabi handed her with a smile and a murmur of thanks. 'Tell me what is happening with Cesar.'

'I don't know,' seemed the safest way forward. Especially as it also had the benefit of being truthful.

'Do you like him?'

'Yes…' Hearing the doubt in her own voice, she shrugged. 'I do like him, but I still don't feel as if I know him. We see each other in public, we're on show. Sometimes I wonder if Cesar is always on show. Always diplomatic, a smile and the right word always to hand.'

'I think that is how the princes here are, be they Casavallian or Aguilarean. They mask their emotions; Cesar perhaps even more so than Luca and Antonio. According to Luca, Cesar's parents were even more distant than Vincenzo and Maria. But I think the real Cesar is worth knowing. Luca likes him.'

'He's easy to like,' Gabi said, heard the slight undertone of bitterness. 'He has that natural royal charm that I lack. I'm so…rough around the edges. And the press, the publicity—I find it so hard to deal with. It feels like everyone is waiting for me to do something wrong and sometimes whatever I do is wrong. So, I can't win.'

Imogen leant forward, her blue eyes full of both sympathy and empathy. 'It is such early days. The princes have had their whole lifetime in the spotlight; they've learnt how to handle it. As will you. And if anyone can help with that, Cesar can.'

'Sometimes I wonder whether I should simply have stayed home, in Crystal Lake.'

Her friend's forehead creased in a frown of concern. 'You don't really mean that, do you?'

'No. I guess not. Sometimes, though, it all feels a bit much.'

'Perhaps you should think about making the final cut and sell the book store.'

'Sell it?' Panic flared. Her book store was her safety net; her back-up plan. The safe haven she still fantasised about a return to.

'Yes. Give someone else the opportunity you thrived on. To make it theirs. Because, in truth, are you really going to go back?'

Gabi shook her head. 'I don't know, Imogen. It could be that in the end I do stand aside, if the people truly revolt. Then Luca will end up on the throne.'

Imogen shook her head. 'That won't happen. Luca believes it is yours by right and he will do all he can to ensure you become Queen. In fact, there is an idea I would like to talk to you about.'

'What idea?'

'Luca feels that his presence here is harming you— it is a reminder to people that he was once heir. But he still wants to show his support to you and Casavalle. He wondered if you would consider him taking on an ambassadorial role abroad for a while.'

'When?' Gabi struggled to keep her voice steady; the idea of losing her brother and her best friend caused tears to threaten but she knew she had to consider this as a ruler.

'Soon. The plan is to go away for a while now, perhaps get it all set up, and then return for your coronation.'

'You don't need my permission; I want you and Luca to be happy so, of course, if this is what he wants, I agree.' And it was the right path—after all, Imogen had always wanted to travel and this would give Luca a chance to experience a whole new life. But the sadness persisted and for some reason an image of Cesar came to mind. A realisation that if she didn't marry him, he too would leave. Return to his ambassadorial duties. And she wasn't sure she wanted him to go. She raised her wine glass. 'To new beginnings,' she stated.

'And old friendships,' Imogen said.

And the two best friends clinked glasses.

Cesar tried to focus on the report; try as he might he kept seeing Gabi's face instead of the diplomatic words on the paper. A face that looked a little pinched and a little shadowed under the expert make-up. She was playing her part but he could sense her tension, how much it cost her to do so.

Being royal was tough, and she would have to learn how to carry the mantle but, dear Lord, her vulnerability didn't sit well with him; he didn't like to see the doubts in those beautiful brown eyes and didn't like the knowledge he was responsible for some of them.

He looked up at the knock on the door and blinked as Luca Valenti walked in, his face dark. 'What exactly are you playing at, Cesar? With my sister?'

Cesar raised his eyebrows. 'Hello to you too, Luca.' He and Luca got on, but right now Luca was clearly in protective brother mode and Cesar didn't blame him.

Perhaps if he, Cesar, had been a better brother to Meribel, much scandal could have been averted.

'Spare the diplomatic words, Cesar. You will not charm your way out of this one.'

'I do not wish to charm my way out of anything. Sit down. Tell me the problem.'

'What are your plans for Gabi?'

'That is private between Gabi and myself.'

'I do not want to see my sister hurt.'

'I would never hurt Gabriella. For that you have my word. But I will not discuss our relationship with you.'

'I understand that and I believe that you do not intend to hurt Gabi. But please remember that I did not intend to hurt Meribel.' Luca's voice was fierce with truth. 'I would have sworn the same to you.'

'Point taken and understood and I repeat: I will not hurt Gabriella.'

'Then why does she look so tired? She will not talk to either myself or Imogen about it and my mother simply tells me to leave be. That Gabriella is a grown woman.'

'Your mother is a wise woman.' Though Luca was right, Gabriella did look tired and Cesar needed to do something about it. He sat back and for a moment the two men regarded each other. Then Cesar repeated. 'I will not hurt her.' After all, he couldn't; that was the beauty of not bringing love into the mix. Because where there was no love, there could be no hurt.

Cesar watched as Luca considered and then he nodded. 'You will answer to me if you do.'

'Understood. Now relax, have a beer. Tell me your plans.'

And so the two men settled down to talk.

CHAPTER NINE

THE NEXT MORNING Cesar entered the Casavallian palace—
at Gabriella and Queen Maria's behest he now had the run
of the grounds and was an accepted presence. But today
was the first time he had entered the royal kitchens and
there was a buzz of interest at his appearance.

The head chef approached and Cesar smiled at the
man known only as Marcello, a chef famed throughout the land, rivalled only by the royal chef Davina of
Aguilarez.

'Good morning, Marcello.'

'Your Royal Highness. How may I be of help?'

'First can I congratulate you on your *pasta con le
sarde* at the ambassadorial lunch? It was perfect.'

The chef beamed at him.

'Next I was wondering if I could take Princess Gabriella's trolley to her this morning.'

'Of course. It is nearly ready. The papers have been
delivered.'

'But first I would like to make a small adjustment. I
know she usually has tea but today I would like to make
her something different. But I need your help.'

Ten minutes later, Cesar reached the library, knocked
and entered.

'Thank you, Bened—' Gabi broke off as she saw who had entered, and a smile lit her face, a smile she quickly suppressed.

'Oh. I wasn't expecting you.'

'But you are pleased to see me.' His smile held satisfaction and her eyes narrowed, though whether in annoyance with herself or him he wasn't sure. 'I am pleased to see you too,' he offered as he pushed the trolley closer to where she was curled up in an armchair. 'And I have brought you this.'

'What is it?'

She eyed the tall mug and turned to him with a question in her eyes.

'It is a double-double,' he explained. He had done some research and, according to Luca, both Imogen and Gabriella loved this type of coffee, made with cream and sugar at a well-known Canadian outlet. 'As near to authentic as possible, though Marcello has given it the Marcello touch.'

Gabi blinked, raised a hand to her eye and then picked up the mug. 'Thank you. That is really thoughtful.' Another blink. 'Enough to make me cry.' But then a look of weariness touched her eyes and she glanced at the door. 'Will I need to pose for the press over this romantic gesture?'

'No.' In truth that hadn't even occurred to him; the realisation pinged a small message of worry before he dismissed it. A cup of coffee was hardly newsworthy. 'I just wanted to cheer you up.'

But he realised that she was no longer listening. Instead her eyes were riveted to the pile of newspapers on the trolley.

Reaching out, she picked up the topmost one. 'What the…?'

Cesar watched as she read, saw the colour leech from her face, and then she looked up and he saw anger sparkle in her brown eyes.

'Show me.' He held out a hand and she put the paper in it, keeping her eyes on him as he scanned the article.

Wake up and smell the roses! And I don't mean a romantic bouquet!

In the past week speculation and rumour has been rife about the 'budding' romance—see what I did there?—between Princess Gabriella of Casavalle and Prince Cesar of Aguilarez. And romance does seem to be blooming—which has made everyone forget that in mere weeks Princess Gabriella plans to take the throne of Casavalle.

Now, some may claim she is an impostor—but this is technically untrue. DNA and legal proof show that she is indeed the late King Vincenzo's rightful heir. Morally speaking, though…it is a different matter.

Let's look at the facts.

Fact: Princess Gabriella's mother, Sophia Ross, left King Vincenzo whilst she was pregnant, without telling him of the pregnancy—if we're speaking of morality here, this is not moral.

Fact: The divorce was apparently requested very soon after her flight—King Vincenzo still didn't know of the pregnancy.

Fact: King Vincenzo granted the divorce just weeks after the birth of Gabriella, a child he didn't know about.

Fact: If he had known he would have granted the divorce as soon as it was requested and Gabriella would not be his heir.

Even putting aside these facts as easily as Prince Luca seems to have put aside his duties and the throne, we have to question whether Gabriella Ross is fit to be Queen.

This is a woman with zero training in royal duties, who is the daughter of a woman who had no respect for or understanding of royalty.

How can Gabriella be Queen? What if she follows in her mother's footsteps and does a runner when it all becomes too much...? As, of course, it will. Especially if this romance withers and dies.

So, wake up, Gabriella. Smell the Casavallian roses and then go home.

To Canada.

Cesar read to the end and then looked across to where Gabi now paced the library floor, coffee in hand. 'I wouldn't take it too personally.'

'How can I not take that personally? She is saying I'm not up to the job and she has twisted the facts to make my mother sound like a terrible irresponsible person and she wasn't. I can't let her get away with it.'

'There is nothing you can do. Responding to these articles simply makes it worse. You must read and move on.'

'I can't.' There was a crack in her voice and he rose to his feet, headed towards her, took her hands in his and for the first time ever, he felt an urge to call out a journalist, to make her think about the effect of her words.

'I hate that they are speaking about my mother with so little sympathy. I hate that they are judging me.'

'This article is one woman's interpretation. She did not know your mother. She does not know you.' His eyes searched hers for clues. 'The past months there have been so many articles, so many stupid assertions, ill-conceived, ill-informed opinions in the press. You have ignored them all.' But perhaps each one had taken its toll, seeped its insidious poison into a woman who was not used to the horrific glare or the ravenous insatiability of public interest.

She inhaled a deep audible breath and straightened her shoulders. 'You're right. Of course, I need to ignore it.'

But he could still see the hurt in her eyes, sense the effort it had taken to say the words. There was nothing he could do about that; it simply came with the territory and Gabriella would learn to deflect the negativity with time. So he should let it be now…but he couldn't. Because he suspected there was more to it than she was admitting, because he wanted to see the defeated look in her eyes vanish. 'Or you can tell me why this article has hit such a nerve.'

'I…'

He tightened his hands round hers. 'Maybe I can help.'

'I don't think you can. Have you ever felt that you can't do something? Felt helpless, unsure?'

He recalled the helplessness that bombarded his senses when he saw first-hand the tragedies and the poverty, the senseless violence and the unrest in the world. The frustration he felt when he realised that his parents could only see what was good for Aguilarez, didn't particularly care about the 'bigger picture' he'd tried to explain. When they had vetoed many of his ideas for their country to be more of a force for good.

'Yes,' he said, now. 'I have. Truly I have.'

For a long moment she studied his face, perhaps read the sincerity there.

'Is that how you feel now?' he asked.

'Yes. It is. What if she is right?' Her voice was small now, tired, almost defeated. 'Everything she says is true. I have no training, no innate understanding of how royalty works. At my presentation ball I know I shocked at least four important personages; every day there is an article that snips or snipes at me. For being too direct. Too Canadian. For not grasping protocol. For usurping my brother's throne. For being my mother's daughter. So what if that article is right? Maybe morally I should stand aside.'

'We discussed this—you seemed sure that you had made the right decision, that your brothers and the Queen wished for you to rule.'

'They do, because they believe that it is technically and morally the right choice, the honourable choice. But that doesn't mean I can do it. And I know that if I stood aside Luca would be an incredible ruler. Perhaps I made the wrong choice, for the wrong reasons. I was so happy to have a family. Perhaps it clouded my judgement.'

Still holding her hands, he tugged gently and led her to an opulent sofa, urged her to sit and sat next to her, twisted his body so he could see her face. Momentarily distracted by the closeness of her, that vanilla scent, the amber flecks in her brown eyes, he blinked to focus himself. 'If Luca thought you could not rule, if he thought you would be bad for Casavalle, he would not have relinquished his claim.'

'But what if he is wrong? What if he is seeing what he wants to see?' The anguish in her voice tore at his chest and for the first time he truly began to understand the enormity of what had happened to her. The extent of the upheaval, the impact on her life.

'I absolutely believe you can do this. In fact I believe you are exactly what Casavalle needs. A breath of fresh air, someone who has not been brought up with all our stuffy rules and traditions. Perhaps you can instil some new traditions of your own.'

'Really?' Her eyes lit up slightly with a sparkle of hope.

'Really. But it has to be what you want to do. This is a job for life, a role that requires wholehearted commitment to your country and its people.'

'I know.' She closed her eyes, then opened them again. 'I'm sorry, Cesar. I didn't mean to fly into such a fuss.' She hesitated. 'I am just a bit emotional. Imogen told me yesterday that she and Luca are leaving Casavalle.'

Cesar nodded. 'I have spoken with Luca and believe he would make an excellent advocate for you and your country.'

'I know. But…'

'But you will lose your brother and your best friend.' Cesar could see the pain in her eyes, knew too that she wouldn't have shown it to either Luca or Imogen.

'Yes.' Now she smiled, a smile that tugged at his heart strings with its bravery. 'I am pleased for them but it has made me feel very alone.'

'You don't have to be alone,' he said, the words falling from his lips instinctively, imbued with an emotional depth and a meaning that caused caution to rear its head. This was not about emotions; this was about practicality.

She didn't need to be alone; they could work together. He could offer the practical support that she needed. 'You could marry me.' Seeing her brown eyes meet his in question, he hurried on. 'I am not trying to take advantage of a moment of weakness.'

'Is that what you think this is? A moment of weakness?' Now anger sparked her eyes and voice; she pulled her hands away and rose to her feet.

The question stopped him in his tracks. Did he believe that—that to show emotion was weakness? It was a question he wasn't sure he wanted to analyse. 'That came out wrong. I simply wanted to say that as your husband I would be able to offer you support, make the task of ruling less lonely.' The words stilted and he saw her expression change, close down to cool neutrality.

'I'll bear it in mind.' Her tone was even. 'And I'm sorry for letting emotion get the better of me. It's foolish. I know it is better for Luca and Imogen to go. Just as I know whatever I do the press will find some angle to pillory me for. I guess I need to grow up and figure out how to be royal.'

Again Cesar knew he should applaud the words, laud the mask he could see her layer on. Yet instead he felt like a first-class horse's backside. Felt he'd lost something that he wanted back.

Stupid.

He needed to think practically—Gabriella was a woman on the edge and that was not good when right now her every action would be under scrutiny, when more articles were bound to spew forth the closer to her coronation it got. A plan began to form in the recesses of his mind.

CHAPTER TEN

GABI RESISTED THE urge to yawn, managed to swallow down the tiredness, focused on keeping her eyes wide open and an expression of interest on her face. In normal circumstances she would be interested; the official was explaining the tax system in Casavalle and how it impacted on the people. Whilst tax wasn't exactly her hobby horse, she did want to get her head around the economics of normal people's normal lives in this country, versus what she had known back home. Wanted a good standard of living for everyone.

But today it all felt too much. She was surrounded by officials and courtiers and staff and even family and yet she felt more alone than ever. A loneliness she must conceal. No more moments of weakness. Instead she forced her tired brain to focus. Smiled at the official. 'I truly appreciate your time and your patience. I will read all these documents and I am sure I will come back to you with further questions.'

The grey-haired man positively beamed at her. 'Thank you, ma'am, for listening so attentively and I look forward to further discussions.'

Once the man had left, Gabi yawned discreetly, stretched and tried to recall what the next official en-

gagement was. She turned to face the door at the sound
of the turn of the handle, royal smile back in place.

'Cesar?' Her heart gave a little hop, skip and jump—it
clearly hadn't caught up with the fact that this man would
deem such a reaction a *physical* weakness, no doubt. She
frowned. Surely she wasn't supposed to see him until an
official dinner the following evening.

'Surprise,' he said.

Gabi had no idea where he was going with this so
contented herself with silence.

'I'm whisking you away,' he announced.

Huh? 'I don't understand.'

He entered the room and stood in front of her. 'I have
cleared your schedule and I am taking you away from
it all,' he announced with a theatrical flourish. 'On a
Christmas break. It is a week until Christmas. I would
like you to visit my country and see some of the Christmas traditions of Aguilarez. You need a break. Some
time out.'

'But...'

'No buts. I have cleared it all with the Queen.'

'But... I haven't even packed.'

'All sorted. We are leaving now.' Gabi tried to get her
brain to assess the situation but it was simply too tiring.
The idea of a break made her whole body tingle with
relief. The idea of a break with Cesar made her whole
body tingle. Full stop.

'Where are we going?'

'To a royal residence in Aguilarez. The car's waiting outside.'

Gabi felt a giddy sense of anticipation as she rose to
her feet; this was really happening. 'There are also photographers waiting outside,' Cesar said and a tiny dart of

disappointment quivered. Of course this was a publicity stunt, part of the romance illusion. No doubt Cesar had upped his game in response to the article of the previous day and she should be grateful for that. Or perhaps her moment of weakness had made him think it was expedient to whisk her away before she actually ran away. As her mother had.

As if he read her mind his lips twisted in a grimace. 'I have done a deal with them. In return for a few smiles now and the promise of a future story they will leave us be for a few days. I can't guarantee utter press blackout but it will be easier.'

'Thank you.' God, how she wished she could read his mind, see underneath the diplomacy. Figure out if all of this was a cool, calculated attempt to persuade her to marry him or whether he cared. *Whoa. Careful, Gabi.* It was a pointless question and she shouldn't care about the answer. Caring didn't come into it, other than the basic respect and liking that Cesar had offered her.

She followed him to the car, held his hand and smiled with what she hoped was a regal yet love-dazed expression on her face.

Once the vehicle had set off at a smooth glide, Cesar glanced at her and said, 'Why don't you take the opportunity to sleep?'

The idea was tempting but she knew she wouldn't be able to do it—would be too worried she might snore or drool or say something mad in her sleep. Especially if Cesar Asturias should venture into her dreams. She glanced at his handsome face, the cool features, and decided instead to take this opportunity to try and find out something about him. Maybe even get some insight into who this man was. She'd caught glimpses but it was as if he guarded himself so well he had forgotten who he was.

'I'm fine but I'd like to use this break to get to know each other better, so maybe we should start now. Perhaps you could tell me a bit about your job, about your life these past years.'

His stance was relaxed but she sensed a hint of wariness. 'I'm an ambassador. I promote Aguilarez. I make sure we play our part on the world stage. We may be small but we are still significant. Both our countries are. Our tourist trade is booming. We also export wines and olives and, of course, people are always interested in our royal family.'

'Do you enjoy it? That first night you said that sometime it chafes to be what you have been preordained to be.'

'I should not have said that. My job is one that I enjoy and am good at. It also brings all the perks of an enjoyable lifestyle.'

Gabi frowned, sensed that what he said was true but that there was another stratum beneath the words. 'There's something you aren't telling me.'

Cesar looked as though he sincerely wished she had opted to take a nap. 'Not at all,' he said lightly. 'It's a great job, hard work but fun as well. Of course, there are some frustrations.'

'Such as.'

'Being royal has its disadvantages. People are always more interested in my latest relationship or which star-studded party I may attend next, or what my family is up to. There is also the fact that I have to always remember I am a mouthpiece for the Asturias clan. But these are simply minor inconveniences.'

No. It was more than that—she wasn't sure how she knew, but she did. Could detect a bitter tinge to the flavour of the words. She regarded him thoughtfully. 'More interested in your relationships than in what? And does that mean that sometimes you have different views from your family?'

'I didn't say that. I think you may be overanalysing here.'

'That's a polite way to tell me to mind my own beeswax.' But suddenly she didn't want to as frustration and a dollop of anger hit her. 'Fine, but over these past days I have talked to you. About topics I care about. You have given me nothing but facts; I have no idea what you care about. Except your duty to your country.'

'Maybe there is nothing else.'

'I don't believe that and I need to know something more...personal about you. How can I contemplate marriage to someone who sees life through a filter of detachment?'

There was a silence.

Then he shrugged. 'OK. You were right. There are times when I would like to speak out about things I do care about, that aren't connected to Aguilarez. About humanitarian aid, about trying to make the world a better place, not just privileged countries like mine. I have travelled in my ambassadorial duties to places where I have cried at the plight of children and families. Seen sights I would not have believed possible in war-torn countries... And, yes, I would like my country to do more, give more humanitarian aid. I would like to be deployed more to those countries, perhaps in a different capacity. But my father decided I would serve Aguilarez better in my current role.'

He said the words with almost clinical dispassion and she sensed he hadn't wanted to say them at all. Yet it didn't take away from the undercurrent of sincere, palpable feeling underneath the layer of civility and she wondered exactly how bitter his disappointment had been.

'That must have been hard—it sounds as though it meant a lot to you.'

'It did. But I see my father's viewpoint and I see little point in defiance—that would not help my cause. Instead I did persuade him to agree to some increased foreign aid, and I do what I can in a different way. I influence decisions and sometimes I go on anonymous trips funded by myself in an unofficial capacity.'

Gabi felt a warmth swell over her, and her mind whirled with the information. It hadn't occurred to her that Cesar would have a charitable side, such a serious side, and there was no doubt that he was serious. There was a set to his lips she hadn't seen before and it gave her a sudden thrill to know that he had such a depth to his character.

But she could also tell he regretted the confidence, had given more than he'd meant.

'Not many people are aware of what I have told you and I would appreciate it if it goes no further.'

'Of course. Thank you for telling me.'

'Also—' he frowned now '—please do not get this out of perspective. I have no complaints. My role is Aguilarez ambassador, not a humanitarian. I do what I can but it is not a life mission for me.'

Gabriella frowned, could almost hear the sound of the diplomatic back-pedalling. Wondered if in truth he preferred to keep that caring side of himself locked down and hidden away even from himself. Whatever it was she smiled now, reached across and brushed a kiss on his cheek. 'I think the fact that you care is incredible, something to be proud of.'

Big mistake. Not the words but the action. The feel of his skin against her lips, the closeness of him, the desire to 'miss' her aim and target his lips nigh on impossible to resist. But somehow resist it she did. Scooted across the seat and looked out of the window, realised the car had started a steep ascent up a rocky, mountainous path.

'Nearly there,' Cesar stated with a slightly over-the-top breeziness and she figured he would be as relieved as she was to arrive. 'Keep looking. That way you get the full effect.'

The car continued to climb, curved round a bend in the narrow road and Gabi gave a gasp as their destination appeared. The mini castle was incredible; it loomed into view with a magnificent beauty. It looked as though it had been carved into the mountain, a fortress-like creation that called to mind the force of nature combined with the power of man.

'It's like a smaller version of the main palace,' Cesar said.

As the car drew up Gabi's eyes widened at the sight of the gardens. Exotic green shrubs, immense trees weighted with a layer of snow and ornate gilded water fountains that rocketed streams of water into the air where they glistened in the late morning sun. Made the whole into a magical winter's spectacle.

The driver opened the door and she climbed out with a murmur of, 'Thank You, Lorenzo.' Then followed Cesar through the arched splendour of the door and into a cavernous hallway, the stone walls hung with tapestries that glowed with a lustre that made the scenes seem to come alive as she studied them. Battles, everyday life, people and actions from centuries before.

Next he led her into a huge oak-panelled room. A roaring fire sent out swathes of welcome heat; the flames flickered and danced in a glow of red and orange and yellow. The whole scene was so welcoming and cosy her whole being basked in the warmth of it all.

There was a huge sofa scattered with cushions; a fluffy rug of enormous proportions covered the hearth. The whole room was redolent of polished woods and varnished history to be seen in the portraits and landscapes on the walls, and she loved it. Then she saw a basket of books by the sofa, some from her keeper shelf, others brand new.

She turned to Cesar in question.

'I brought them from the place and some new ones Imogen said you may like. I thought maybe what you'd like is some time to curl up by a fire and read.'

Gabi turned to him, felt a sudden glisten of tears.

'How did you know that?'

'Lucky guess.' Only it wasn't. It was because he'd listened to her over the past days, really listened. And now her gaze went to the tree in the corner—a Christmas tree, huge, luxuriant, and as yet undecorated.

Cesar looked a little embarrassed. 'This is just an idea. You said that you missed decorating a tree this year so I thought, well, maybe we could decorate this one. Obviously you don't have to.'

'I'd love to.' Gabi eyed the tree. 'But we'll need a lot of decorations.'

'I thought we could go and buy some. The nearest town has a Christmas market. If we go this afternoon and we wrap up so we look inconspicuous I doubt anyone will recognise us. Because no one will have figured out where we are yet. We have the place to ourselves. My housekeeper will pop in with supplies but otherwise we are going to fend for ourselves.'

Without the trappings of royalty, not even a skeleton staff. Just them. Her heart skipped a little. 'Then let's go. Show me to my room and I will get myself disguised in the twinkle of an eye.'

'Hold on. To complete the disguise.'

She grinned as she saw what he held out. A pot of bright red nail polish. 'Perfect. I'll see if I can think of any more royal protocols to break.'

To her own surprise her tiredness had melted away, replaced by an anticipatory buzz of…happiness. *Careful, Gabi.* No, for this break she didn't want to be careful. It was OK to be happy—for a few days she would be free of royal rules and duties. She wanted, needed, to make the most of it.

Cesar glanced down at Gabi as they walked through the medieval town, over the ancient cobbled streets, thronged now with Christmas crowds. Chatter and laughter hummed on the air, redolent with the scent of spiced wine and Christmas delicacies.

'This is magical,' Gabi breathed, gesturing upwards at the glittering, sparkling illumination of the Christmas lights that looped and twinkled overhead in an array of stars. A reflection of the sky itself.

'Yes,' he agreed, and realised he didn't mean the setting, beautiful though it was. He meant her—she looked relaxed and happy, her lips curved up in a generous smile, her eyes sparkling as she enjoyed the atmosphere and bit into the enormous pretzel he'd bought for her.

The fluffy red hood completely hid her chestnut hair and also shielded her face from passers-by, and, dressed simply, she blended into the crowds. Cesar wore a woollen hat and had also wrapped a scarf round the lower half of his face. They looked, in fact, like any other couple out to do some Christmas shopping and the security detail were discreet enough to be virtually indistinguishable from the crowds.

They approached the cluster of stalls that made up the market, each one displaying goods and wares that caught the senses. Bright woollen garments, delicacies and pastries, *glühwein* and marshmallows and hot chocolate. And Christmas decorations.

Gabi lingered over the choice and Cesar took the chance to watch her, the care with which she examined each trinket, the concentration on her face as she debated colour schemes. 'We could go for a blaze of colour or we could keep it simple. What do you think?'

'I really don't mind. What do you normally do?'

'Normally I try to do a theme around a book. Christmas books mostly, though I did do a wizard theme one year.'

'That sounds hard.'

'It was a bit. But I enjoyed it—I really did. It was worth it to see the kids' faces when they came in. And I'd always hang little wrapped chocolates on there as well. Because kids deserve to have a magical Christmas.' Her eyes fell on a young couple with a family nearby, absorbed in the study of a nativity scene. 'Like them. You can see the love there and the magic of Christmas.' The dark-haired woman leant down to listen to what her daughter said, dropped a kiss on her head, and the father lifted his son up to show the toddler something and beamed as the little boy pointed in excitement.

Seeing the sadness in her eyes, Cesar knew that she was thinking of the loss of her mother. 'And adults deserve the same. So this next two days will be devoted to Christmas magic.'

The sadness vanished and there was her beautiful smile again. 'Then let's make the tree a magical one. We'll go for white and gold and make it the kind of tree that you'd find in a fairy tale. Let's go and decorate.'

CHAPTER ELEVEN

'RIGHT,' SAID GABRIELLA. 'We need a plan. The lights have to go on first, then the tinsel.'

'I am completely in your hands,' Cesar said, and revelled in the blush that touched her cheeks. A satisfaction that morphed into a desire to kiss her, an urge that was hard to deny. If she married him, of course, then they would be able to kiss whenever they wanted, the idea both scary and wonderful. Scary enough to cause him to focus on winding the lights around the tree.

The next hour was…fun, he realised when, breathlessly, they surveyed the end result of their efforts. The tree swirled with magic, illuminated by the white lights that twinkled and glinted, the gold ornaments lit by the flames of the fire. The whole creation was topped by a star of multi-faceted crystalline beauty.

'One last thing,' he said.

Gabi turned to him in question and then her face broke into a smile as he pulled a box out of one of the shopping bags.

'Chocolates,' he explained. 'To hang on the tree. For us.' He glanced at the tree slightly guiltily. 'As long as it doesn't spoil the overall pattern.'

'Chocolate can never spoil anything. Thank you. This

was really thoughtful.' For a second he held his breath. Half hoping, half terrified that she would kiss him again. His cheek still tingled from the butterfly kiss she'd given him in the car.

She stepped forward and then back again as if common sense had overcome desire; perhaps she too had the same breathless, heady sense of nerves.

'You're welcome.' He gestured to the sofa. 'Come and sit down and survey the splendour of our creation and I'll go get us some hot chocolate.'

Gabi stared into the flames, watched as they leapt and danced to the crackle of the logs. For the first time in such a long time she felt relaxed...normal, and it was wonderful. And all thanks to Cesar. She looked up as he re-entered the lounge, bearing two large steaming mugs.

'That smells divine.'

'I've put in a secret ingredient—a shot of rum.'

He sat next to her and the reassuring bulk of his body felt warm and cosy and intimate as they both watched the twinkle of the Christmas lights on the tree.

'Thank you. It was lovely to decorate a tree with someone again.'

'You said you used to decorate with your aunt?'

'Yes. The first Christmas after my mom died Aunt Bea took me to buy tree decorations. I was only four but the memory is really clear. I think it was the first time Aunt Bea had bought so many decorations. To be honest I don't think they bothered with a tree before they took me in. After that we used the same decorations every year—even when they got tatty, I insisted. In my head they were somehow traditional, connected with my mother and family.' Gabi swallowed a sudden lump in her throat; decorating the tree had been a time when she had felt truly close to her aunt. She could still remember the way the elderly woman had followed the ritual every year, pushing her glasses up her nose every time she stood back to check on their progress. 'After they died, I couldn't bring myself to do it any more. I decorated the tree in the book store instead.'

'You must have missed them very much.'

'I did—I still do. Right after they died I felt so... alone in the world. Orphaned all over again. I don't really remember much of my mother, but I do remember a warmth, a sense of safety and love that I associate with her. And I also remember the utter confusion, the bewilderment I felt when she died. I was too little to comprehend what it meant. But Aunt Bea and Uncle Peter were there for me.' At such a personal cost. 'And I will always be grateful for that. It's good to talk about them.' Something she seldom had the opportunity to do.

'Tell me about them.'

Gabi hesitated—wondered if the crackle of the flames, the absolute marvel of being alone with no staff, no schedule, no expectations, no publicity had gone to her head. Or was it the genuine interest in Cesar's eyes. Who knew? But she wanted to share some of her life with him.

'Uncle Peter was my mother's older brother. Half-brother, in fact, and he was much older than her. Nearly thirty years; they weren't close at all. He was already in his late fifties when my mother left Casavalle, and he was in his sixties when she died. He and my Aunt Bea had no children through choice. I think I...bewildered them.' She was tempted to confide it all—that overheard conversation, the fact that they had given up their dreams for her, but she didn't. Knew her aunt and uncle had never wanted her to know, wary too that Cesar might see the revelation and its impact on her as an emotional moment of weakness. 'But they did their best.' Just as Cesar had promised to do as a father. 'They bought the book store, started a whole new career, made sure I got a good education, taught me so much. And I will always be grateful for that.'

'They sound like good people,' he said softly. 'The times you have described with them are good memories. They spent time with you, you cooked together, walked together, gave each other gifts, decorated a tree together...they encouraged your love of books.'

Now she could see the shadowed pain in his eyes, knew he was remembering his own childhood where his own parents had spent minimal personal time with him.

Her heart bled for the young Cesar, bred through duty not love, and then treated as a royal pawn rather than a little boy, and she shifted towards him. Said nothing because she sensed sympathy or pity would be anathema to him, hoped that somehow her closeness would convey understanding.

They sat like that for a timeless moment, and then he turned and smiled at her. 'I wish I could have met your aunt and uncle. Thank you for sharing your memories.' He rose to his feet. 'Now I think it's time for dinner. Wait here and I will get it.'

'We're going to eat here?'

'Yes.' His expression looked unsure. 'Unless you'd prefer to sit at a table. I thought you'd appreciate as much informality as possible.'

Again a funny warmth touched her. Again she wished she knew if this was a ploy or real. Or whether it actually mattered.

* * *

Ten minutes later Cesar re-entered the lounge, pushing a trolley forward. Two plates covered with silver-domed cloches. 'Here we are,' he announced as he approached the sofa and removed the covers with a flourish.

Gabi broke into a delighted peal of laughter. 'Pizza!' she exclaimed.

'But not any old pizza. This is Aguilarean pizza. The base is sourdough and the olives are home grown and the tomato sauce is a state secret. Truly, you will never have eaten pizza like this.' He handed her her plate, picked up his own and sat down next to her.

Gabi gave a small exhalation of pure satisfaction. 'No cutlery in sight,' she murmured. 'Perfect. Finger food I can manage.' She took her first bite, closed her eyes in appreciation and Cesar felt his own lips curve into a smile even as desire tugged inside him. 'This is incredible. Why haven't I tried this before?'

'I don't know. You could go and request pizza from the Casavallian kitchens, but it wouldn't be as good. Or better yet go in person and ask.'

'I wouldn't dare!' Gabi looked horrified. 'They are so busy and they terrify me. Plus I'm not sure Maria would like it.'

'Maria is a wonderful woman and an excellent queen, but she is a different person from you. You need to do things your way.'

Gabi bit her lip. 'It's not that easy. I have so much to learn; and everyone else knows more than I do about everything.' She picked up another slice of pizza. 'I know that's a bit sweeping but it's true.'

'No. It isn't. I can think of something you know more about.'

'You can?'

'Yes. Books.'

'Right... But I'm not sure that's a great help to ruling.'

'Actually I disagree. You don't just care about books. You told me that you believe everyone should read. That sounds more like a policy in the making than a hobby.'

There was a short pause and her eyes lit up in sudden understanding, sparked into enthusiasm as she stared at him. 'I could promote literacy in Casavalle. I ran classes myself in Crystal Lake, taught people of all ages. Did you know, according to some reports, it is possible that two in five Canadians have low literacy? Sometimes it's because they have undiagnosed dyslexia or they have low attendance due to their home life. And it holds them back all their life—makes it harder to get a job, makes so much of everyday tasks more difficult and deprives them of the sheer pleasure of reading. I am sure that there are people here who have the same difficulties.'

He nodded, touched by the sheer passion and vibe to her voice, the belief in the cause. Lord knew, he understood that.

'You could also speak with my father about the idea of rolling out a similar programme in Aguilarez.'

'Speak with your father?' Her face dropped. 'I... I...'

'He is not a tyrant,' Cesar said. 'He is driven by duty and I believe he will see that this is a worthy cause that will benefit his people. It is just not something that has occurred to him.'

He watched as she tackled another piece of pizza, could almost see her brain whir and process ideas. 'I'll need to talk to my Education minister.'

Cesar hid the small smile as he heard her describe the

minister as 'hers' but, as was her wont, she caught it and smiled right back at him.

'Don't I sound all grand and regal?' she said. 'But, truly, I'm excited about this. I'll need to review the education statistics, look into any charitable foundations that already exist. Call in the people who run them.'

He nodded, sensed her energy and verve. 'Speak with some teachers, find out how much provision is made for children with reading difficulties.'

'And why stop there? I need to think about all children, all people with learning difficulties, mental-health issues.' She waved her pizza. 'Would you mind brainstorming with me?'

'I'd love to,' he said, almost surprised to know he completely meant it.

As they spoke and swapped ideas over the rest of the pizza, followed by chocolate ice-cream, the atmosphere seemed to crackle and buzz in time with the sizzle of the logs on the fire, the pop of the flames in the air. And gradually, as the words began to run dry, awareness grew as he observed the animation on her face, the gesture of her hands, the brightness of her eyes, her sheer vitality.

Until the words seemed to slow down and finally trickled to a stop and he realised just how close Gabriella was—so very, very close... And as if she realised the same she stilled, and her brown eyes widened as their gazes caught.

He knew he had to say something and the words came naturally. 'The more I get to know you, the more I believe you are the exact ruler Casavalle needs. You bring a change of attitude, because you have experienced life as a non-royal and you bring a different perspective. You will be a great queen.'

'Do you really think so?' Her voice held shyness, doubt, but a growing confidence as well.

'Yes.' He kept his voice steady, willing her to believe the words. 'I really do.'

Now there was a silence, but this silence echoed and reverberated with unsaid words, unnecessary words as mutual yearning hovered and meshed the very air and drew them towards each other until now the gap between them was infinitesimal. Then Gabriella closed that gap, and brushed her lips against his. Cesar released the breath he hadn't even known he held, and he lifted his hands, threaded them through the silken mass of her hair. The tang of dark chocolate, the scent of her vanilla shampoo, assailed his senses and he was lost.

She deepened the kiss, pressed against him with a small moan; her fingers fumbled with the buttons of his shirt, slid over his chest and he groaned her name and then they somehow tumbled off the sofa onto the fleecy softness of the rug, warmed by the flames whilst outside moonlight dappled the stone turrets and the ornate fountains.

A sudden pop of a log penetrated the intense fugue of desire and Gabriella pulled abruptly away, scrambled up to a sitting position and looked down at him, dismay breaking through the dazed look of desire as they stared at each other.

She looked so damned beautiful and guilt fought its way to the surface—he should not have let this happen. 'I'm sorry,' he said. 'I didn't mean to get so carried away.' And he hadn't. That had not been part of his marriage campaign; in truth the campaign hadn't so much as crossed his mind.

She caught her lower lip between her teeth. 'Neither did I. I'm sorry too.'

All he wanted now was to take the stricken look from her face. 'Then we are both sorry, but look at me, Gabi. Please.'

She did so, her gaze half shy, half vulnerable, and he continued, 'I find it hard to regret, because I wanted to kiss you, you wanted to kiss me. What happened here—it wasn't wrong and we were at least saved by the fire from going any further. It is done—let us simply remember it as a beautiful memory, rather than something we regret. Deal?'

A pause and then she nodded. 'You're right. It's a deal,' she said.

CHAPTER TWELVE

GABI OPENED HER EYES, blinked at the unfamiliar canopy
above her, turned her head to see the vast bedroom,
filled with heavy dark furniture, the loom of a mahog-
any wardrobe in the corner, the sharp edges of the ornate
desk by the barred window. Another blink and memories tumbled into her still-sleep-drowsed brain. Had it
all been a dream?

Nope…the feel of Cesar's body pressed against her,
the soft fleece of the rug, the warmth of the fire, his lips
on hers… That had all happened. Lifting her fingers to
touch her swollen lips, she closed her eyes, tried to tell
herself that at least they had come to their senses before
they had actually slept together. That would have been
stupid. Yet, stupid or not, a part of her cursed that falling
log, wished that they had continued that magical journey,
her whole body still alive and alight and wanting more.

Gabi exhaled a sigh———what had happened to not
letting physical attraction fuzz her brain?

Well, it was time to face the music, endure the sheer
awkwardness of the morning after.

And yet when, twenty minutes later, she entered the
cavernous kitchen Cesar turned from the counter and
smiled at her with such an easy, natural smile that the

tension left her shoulders and she even managed a return smile.

'Good morning,' he said. 'I thought we could have breakfast in the morning room and then laze the day away reading in front of the fire.'

The mention of the fire caused a flush to heat her cheeks but she welcomed the plan, was grateful for his aplomb and for the offer of escape into a fictional world. And once she was actually curled up on the rug, close to the warmth of the fire, a cup of tea by her side, she did indeed lose herself in the pages and watched with satisfaction as Cesar did the same. His absorption was genuine—she could see that from the way his dark eyes focused, the steady pace at which he turned the pages, the fact his tea was left untouched as he read the classic fantasy adventure that she'd hoped he loved as much as she did.

The only disturbance was a break for lunch—ciabatta bread with cold meats and regional cheeses—and not long after that his phone rang. He left the room, then popped his head round the door. 'I've got to go out for a bit to pick up some supplies. Keep reading and I'll try not to be gone long.'

But it was a while before he reappeared, and as she looked up at him she saw an expression she couldn't interpret on his face. Excitement? Nerves? It was hard to tell.

'Actually—we're going out,' he said.

'OK.' Gabi slipped her bookmark into the book and closed it. 'Where to? Do I need to change?'

'Just wrap up warm,' he said. 'And meet me outside.'

Fifteen minutes later Gabi ran lightly down the stairs and across the stone floor to the imposing arched front door. Stepping outside, she gave a small gasp of wonder; outside on the snow-covered ground was a sleigh, at the front of which were two of the most beautiful horses she had ever seen. A man in a top hat and tails was seated behind the horses.

Cesar stood to one side. 'Enter,' he said with a bow and she approached the sleigh, and let him help her in, waited as he climbed in after her and pulled the wonderfully fluffy white blanket over them.

'I didn't even realise it had been snowing.'

'Me neither.' He grinned. 'Flavia rang to tell me and it occurred to me that you may like this.'

'I love this.' She gestured to the landscape: the pristine white of the freshly laid snow stark against the green glimpses of the trees, the sky above a dazzling blue, the late afternoon sun glinting down in wintry splendour. The sound of the runners over the snow, the snuffle of the horses—all of it added to the magical feel of the day.

'Thank you. For today and yesterday as well. I needed this break. It's given me new energy, a fresh perspective. Made me feel stronger.' But she knew it wasn't only the break—it was this man sitting next to her, the man who had made her laugh, had helped decorate a tree, had been compassionate and caring and kind.

'I am glad.' He paused. 'In a few minutes we will be at our destination—a place important to Aguilarean history. A woodland glade where legend has it just over two centuries ago the King of Casavalle and the King of Aguilarez met, after a series of bloody and awful battles. They met and decided enough was enough, that the wars were tearing both countries apart and somehow a peace must be brokered. And so it ended, because two rulers trusted each other, against all odds, and put their people's futures above the feuds and wars and greed. And made a truce.'

'A truce that has held to this day.' Gabi felt a shiver of history, a realisation that those two men of long ago were linked to Cesar and herself.

And she sensed, knew, that Cesar had a purpose other than mere sightseeing in taking her here. And now as the sun dipped down over the horizon in a magnificent blaze of red and orange glory and the day slipped into dusk her tummy tightened with nerves, tension, panic, *all* the emotions. Her senses heightened, the pine-scented breeze intensified in scent, the crunch of the horses' hooves echoed in her ears, the feel of the blanket over her legs heavier as the sleigh pulled to a halt.

'Come,' Cesar said. Somehow, she forced her legs to move, alighted from the sleigh and felt a small thrill as he helped her down, his hand round hers. Then he led her across the crisp crunch of snow into a small woodland glade where she stopped as surprise halted her feet.

The trees were festooned with lights and baubles that glittered in the canopied glade to create a magical tableau. Starlight seeped through the branches and dappled the ground, the snow-covered trees with their contrast of dark green and white adding an almost magical sylvan beauty.

Cesar took her hands in his, his grasp firm and sure.

'Gabriella.' Cesar's voice sounded tight, the word came out with an effort, and he cleared his throat, shook his head and smiled at her. 'Sorry. I'm nervous,' he admitted and the admission touched her. 'I want this to be right. Gabriella Ross Valenti, will you marry me? I pledge you my support, my loyalty, my respect and my fidelity. I will stand by you and I will do my very best to be a good father to our children.'

Gabi tried to think, knew that she had to think. This was a huge decision that encompassed the rest of her life, and also impacted on her country. Her mind went to those two kings of long ago. Had they stood right here, weighing each other up, trying to broker a peace and a trust? Could she marry a man without love? The answer was suddenly simple.

Of course, she could. Love would make this too complicated; love had caused a huge amount of difficulty for her mother, had caused her anxiety, despair and, in the end, heartbreak. Maria and Vincenzo's marriage had stood the test of time from start to finish and brought respect, fidelity, loyalty—what more really could she ask for?

Than this prince, whose brown eyes were locked on her face, a man who would give her what he had pledged; she took in his strength, his aura, his sheer certainty.

'Yes,' she said clearly. 'I will marry you, Cesar Asturias.'

He released her hands and now he delved a hand into his pocket. Pulled out a small jeweller's box. He flicked the box open and took the ring out. Gabi held out her hand and he gently slid the ring onto her finger.

She looked down at it, could feel the thud-thud-thud of her heart against her ribcage as she stared down at the ring that represented a commitment so huge. The colours of the stones were a combination of the Casavalle and Aguilarez flags. The ring a reminder that their marriage was an alliance, a proud alliance, and it would be a happy one.

'It's beautiful. Truly beautiful.' And then he kissed

her. This kiss was different; she knew it from the moment his lips touched hers. It was a kiss of affirmation, a statement kiss, and it called up a deep desire, one that tugged and demanded and yearned for more. This was the first of a lifetime of kisses and she shivered as she pressed against him, felt the pull of possession, the realisation that from now on they belonged to each other.

'I think we should get married very soon,' he said. 'What do you think of a Christmas wedding, on the eve of Christmas?'

'Are you serious?'

'Yes. I think it makes sense to marry before your coronation in the new year. And for entirely personal reasons I would like to marry you sooner rather than later.'

She had no problem with that—her insides still positively squirmed with desire. 'Works for me. On both points. But do you think we can organise it in time?'

'As long as you are happy with a smaller, more private ceremony. It will be too late for foreign dignitaries to rearrange their Christmas schedules.'

'But most of them will come to the coronation anyway and I would much prefer a smaller wedding. And we could honeymoon here. Back in the castle.' Spend Christmas Day in front of the tree they had decorated together, lie in front of the fire as husband and wife.

'Then let's make this happen.'

The days that followed were a whirlwind, of publicity, organisation, planning, there was so much to do: a dress to choose, a reception to organise, a guest list to negotiate.

At least, though, the wedding was to be small. The two royal families would of course attend, with the exception of Meribel, who had decided that she didn't want any adverse publicity to spoil her brother's marriage. And not even Cesar's words would budge her. Other than family there were diplomatic friends and colleagues of Cesar, and Gabi had invited Jonas, who managed the book store, and Rachel, an old friend from Crystal Lake, along with her husband, Tom, and baby Ben.

Then finally her wedding day dawned.

Gabi spent the morning almost in a daze as she got ready. There was little point in pretending she had any input. Imogen, Luca, Tia and Antonio had arrived back in Casavalle the previous day and now Imogen and Tia had taken charge. Gabi had attempted to point out she was a grown woman, not a doll, had also suggested that at seven months pregnant maybe Tia should be resting. But this last had been met with a most unladylike snort from Tia herself.

'Compared to waitressing, pregnancy is a doddle. Plus, Antonio spent the whole honeymoon fussing over me.'

'The *whole* honeymoon?' Imogen asked, her eyebrows raised in a suggestive wiggle.

All three women fell into gales of laughter as Tia admitted, 'Well, maybe not quite all. But my point is that I have plenty of energy and I wouldn't miss helping you get ready for the world. I'll just keep the tea coming and I'll be fine.'

Tia's love of a good cup of tea was known by all and so they took turns boiling the kettle as they set to work.

Gabi sat back and let them get on, watched her reflection as she morphed into a bride. Her hair was expertly coaxed into gentle waves that seemed to gloss down to her shoulders in a chestnut waterfall. The make-up was subtle but effective, brought out the depth of brown in her eyes, accentuated the height of her cheekbones.

And then the dress. Gabi had known from the instant she saw it that it was The One. The one that she hoped would stop Cesar in his tracks. It was deceptively simple, long sleeved with an eye-catching wide neckline that cleverly twisted around her shoulders to fall into a low back. The gown was made of a dense weave fabric with a subtle yet distinctive flower motif. The fitted bodice topped a full pleated skirt at the front and a long flowing train at the back.

Now she was ready and there was a tsunami of panic in her tummy; nerves fluttered and curled in waves as the royal party made the short journey across to the Casavallian chapel.

'You ready?' Luca asked as they stood at the doors to the ancient stone church.

'I'm ready.'

They stepped forward and now all she could see was Cesar—he filled her vision as each step took her closer to him, each step matched the breadth and thrum of the swell of music, that seemed to roll and wave in the air in recognition of the moment. Each step so significant, each pound of her heart stronger. He was so goddamn beautiful, this soon-to-be husband of hers, who waited at the altar, a smile lurking on his lips and in his eyes. A smile that encouraged her to keep moving forward. His gaze encompassed her, made her feel as if she were the only woman in the world for him.

For a fraction of an insidious second, she realised that she was—the only Queen of Casavalle in the vicinity. He would be marrying any woman who wore the crown. For a second, she almost faltered, sensed Luca's grip on her arm tighten, oh, so slightly, as if in question. Then she looked at Cesar again, and he gave the smallest, quickest of winks and suddenly it was all OK again. Now she had reached the altar and he smiled down at her; his gaze unfaltering; no hint of doubt flecked the dark chocolate-brown depths.

Next came the vows, made in this historic beautiful church that had seen so many other royal marriages take place. These walls had witnessed so much, joy and pain, life, death, christenings… So many rulers of Casavalle would have been wed here, indeed her own mother must have wed her father here. The idea sent a shiver down her spine.

Cesar spoke each word clearly and she followed his lead, focused on each syllable, until it got to the vow to love and honour and then there was a beat of hesitation, so fleeting she was sure no one but the two of them would have noted it.

Then it was done.

They were husband and wife, wedlocked.

He pushed her veil back and, oh, so gently he kissed her, his lips feather-light and yet so sensuous. Joy and a tremor of desire coursed her veins and she lifted her hand to gently cup his cheek.

The walk back down the aisle was dreamlike—she even thought she saw Maria wipe a tear from the corner of her eye, which surely must be an illusion. As they emerged into the cold, snow-tanged air she looked round at the blue-grey of the sky, the ancient beauty of the churchyard, and all she could think was the word married. She'd got married. Married. *Married.*

Then it was time for the photographs but today she sailed through the usually hated pastime. Because Cesar was next to her, oh, so close, arm around her waist, her hand lightly resting on his chest, and a new awareness dawned, a thrill of anticipation at the night ahead.

An awareness that simmered as they arrived at the reception, held in one of the Casavallian ballrooms, resplendent in Christmas beauty. The flags of Aguilarez and Casavalle fluttered at the doors. The columns and pillars were draped with beautiful white flowers that trailed and garlanded down with fairy-tale beauty and added a tinge of scent to the air.

An enormous table displayed an array of canapés. Gabi had decided against the formality of a sit-down dinner, preferred the idea of allowing people to mingle. Instead she'd asked for tables to be dotted round the room so that people could sit or stand as they pleased.

'I think it's working,' she said to Cesar as they stood together watching their guests as they laughed and talked. Imogen and Luca circulated, making introductions. Antonio and Tia sat with Miles and Grace, all laughing.

'Even my parents look happy,' he agreed, watching King Jorge smile and nod as Imogen spoke to him. 'Clearly Meribel's faults have been forgotten.'

Now that a different Asturias had married a different soon to be ruler of Casavalle.

'Then hopefully Meribel will feel able to attend my coronation and bring Dana with her.'

'Perhaps. But enough of my family. What about you, Gabi? Are you happy? Are you enjoying yourself?'

'I am. I spoke with Jonas as well and I have told him he can have the book store.'

'Are you sure? I know how much it means to you.'

'It does but it would be selfish of me to hang onto it now. I know it was the right choice. My life is here now.'

With you.

She bit the words back, reluctant to show even a hint of sappiness. Instead, 'Now we should mingle.'

Cesar nodded and with a small wave she moved away. As she did so she spotted a tall, willowy blonde woman who was standing watching her, partly shielded by a fluted, flowered pillar. Gabi smiled and then the smile froze into a rictus as she realised the identity of the guest. Lady Amelia Scott-Browne.

How? Why? No way would she have missed the inclusion of Lady Amelia on the guest list. Equally no way could anyone have gatecrashed this venue. Had Cesar asked Lady Amelia? The thought sent an icy jag through her veins. No, of course he wouldn't, or at least not without telling her. Would he? Perhaps in a loveless marriage he assumed it wouldn't matter to her. It shouldn't matter to her. That Lady Amelia was so beautiful, so elegant, so poised, so…

Stop, Gabi.

Right now, it was imperative that she maintain her poise; no hint of scandal could touch this wedding.

Plus, there was no need for the stabs of jealousy she could feel pinprick her whole body. Cesar and Amelia had been history before Gabi came on the scene and she would not allow herself the indulgence of petty jealousy.

It was the future that was important.

It was simply unfortunate that her immediate future obviously involved a conversation with Lady Amelia. But as she approached the other woman, Gabi was careful to keep a friendly smile on her face.

'Your Highness.' Amelia's voice was low, well-modulated and completely cordial. 'I know you must be wondering why I am here. I assure you that Cesar has no idea I am here.'

'I must admit that I'm a little curious, yes.'

'I have come as the guest of Ferdinand Bastillo, one of Cesar's diplomatic colleagues. And *I* must admit I was guilty of a little subterfuge; Ferdinand believes I have Cesar's permission to be here and it is he who convinced your palace secretary to add me to the guest list at the last minute. But I only came because I wished to talk with you.'

'Oh?'

'I do not know how much Cesar told you about "us" but I believe you are entitled to the truth and I couldn't think of another way to speak with you. I know that letters and emails get censored.'

It was true. Gabriella knew how much trouble Miles had got into for passing her original letter on to Maria, knew too how hard it had been for Tia to get in touch with Antonio. She had been forced to simply turn up as Lady Amelia had now.

'Go ahead,' she said, though every instinct told her to cover her ears with her hands and run away.

Lady Amelia nodded. 'I'm not sure if Cesar has been honest with you, and everything I have seen and heard indicates to me that you have fallen in love with him.'

Gabi hesitated—she could hardly tell Lady Amelia that it was all for the camera.

'I…'

The blonde woman gave a trill of laughter. 'I do understand that obviously you had to ham it up for the press but I believe you have really fallen.'

The realisation hit her like a rock dropping from

the chandelier-adorned ceiling. She did love Cesar. Of course she did—now the thought had entered her mind she knew with absolute blinding certainty that it was true. Oh, she'd told herself she understood the rules but her heart, her body, her very soul had been unable to comply with the orders of her brain.

Because love wasn't like that.

It couldn't be forced or coerced to arrive or leave.

Amelia watched her closely, her green eyes full of sympathy. 'And I can't let him play you like that,' she stated. 'Cesar only broke up with me because his parents told him to, so that he would be free to marry you.'

The words and their import slammed into her. It couldn't be true. It couldn't. Could it? Only it could— her brain was in control now, thinking events through with icy logic.

'Did he tell you that?'

'Not in so many words. Cesar is too wily a diplomat for that. He went to Aguilarez for a meeting with his parents and Queen Maria and on his return he broke up with me. Out of the blue.' Lady Amelia's voice held sadness now. 'Next thing I knew I saw the press speculation about you and him. I know I shouldn't have been surprised; Cesar has always been a man to do his duty, so I understood his decision to sacrifice love.'

'Love?' Despite her best intent her voice raised in pitch.

Amelia shrugged. 'Yes. I think it took him by surprise—at the start of our relationship he was very sure about his short-term plans but as time went on... we fell in love.' The words twisted in Gabi's heart, each one a vicious turn of the knife. 'We were so compatible, had so much fun and he knew I would make an excellent diplomat's wife, so he would have been able to marry me with his parents' approval. But then he was called on to marry you.'

Every word rang with the possibility of truth, gelled with everything Cesar had told her, bar the reason for his break-up with Lady Amelia. And Cesar could not have told her that truth; to do so would have scuppered all his chances of making an alliance with Gabi. And also Cesar was a good man—he wouldn't have wanted to hurt her either. But it all made a horrible poisonous sense.

His words echoed in her brain: *'Love brings its own risks, of loss and grief. It complicates life. If we marry you do not need to fear I will fall in love with anyone.'*

Because he already loved Lady Amelia. And who could blame him? She was beautiful, sophisticated and part of his world.

Lady Amelia continued. 'I just wanted you to know; I also wanted to assure you that I will not pursue Cesar. I will not cause scandal. I intend to get on with my life and I wish him well. I wish you both well. But I couldn't bear to see you expose yourself to hurt.'

Too late. Pain gripped her, a deep ache, and she wondered if the whole room could hear the crack of her heart. Perhaps, but that was all the evidence they would get. She would wear the royal mask, as Cesar had advised, as he had taught her. She would be a Queen.

Even as her soul shrivelled with the realisation that history was repeating. Her past echoed into her present and her future. She was a duty and a burden again, as she had been to her aunt and uncle.

But right now she had to put her country and her pride first. As for her love, she had to squeeze that, compact it and hide the knowledge away. No one must ever, ever suspect that she truly loved Cesar.

She smiled at Lady Amelia, a smile as friendly and regal as she could manage. 'I truly appreciate the effort you have gone to, to tell me this, and I am happy to be able to set your mind at rest. Cesar and I understand each other; he has been honest with me and we look forward to a happy and long-lasting union.'

She had no idea whether or not the words even made sense but she was fairly sure they gave nothing away, would hold up to being quoted to the press if it came to it.

The rest of the reception passed in a daze; her head ached as she chattered and laughed and stood with Cesar in a desperate attempt to appear normal. But now her body no longer yearned for the night to come; instead dread and anticipation weighted her tummy. Because come what may she knew she couldn't sleep with Cesar that night. In truth she didn't even know what to do for the best.

CHAPTER THIRTEEN

CESAR HAD WATCHED the conversation between Amelia and Gabi, had known instinctively that something bad had gone down. But there was no way to discover what it was, no way he could risk any speculation or notice by marching over to join the conversation.

Instead he waited until they had finished, then moved towards Gabi.

'Hey,' he said softly. 'All OK?'

'Fine. Why shouldn't it be?' Her voice was calm, a smile tipped her lips—she seemed every millimetre the happy bride. Dammit, she'd learn how to don a mask all too well, almost well enough to fool him.

Almost.

Because as the reception progressed through the speeches, through the laughter and banter and cacophony of good wishes that accompanied them, he knew she was faking, sensed she was more brittle, more edgy, more…elusive.

Yet he was sure no one else would have the least suspicion and her composure, the way she was acting the part of loved-up, happy regal bride, made him feel edgy himself. This was too reminiscent of his own parents' marriage, every public show of affection an act. The idea that his touch now made her uncomfortable was one that caused a cold hand to grip his insides.

Then finally it was time for the bride and groom to leave. Gabi was whisked away by Imogen and Tia to change into her going-away outfit, a simple off-white trouser suit cinched at the waist with a glittering belt, her shoulders covered with a faux-fur shrug. Cesar received a clap on the shoulder from Antonio, a hug from Luca.

'Look after her,' his new brother-in-law murmured.

More hugs from Imogen and Tia; his parents wished them well with cool hauteur, but at least accompanied by smiles.

The car journey back to Aguilarez, achieved in stilted silence, was laden with a sense of foreboding. Sadness touched Cesar along with trepidation—this was not how it was supposed to be. The day had started with such beauty and happiness—he would never forget the sight of Gabriella headed towards him down the aisle, stunning in her radiance.

Now he could see pain and tiredness etched on her face and all he wanted to do was make it go away. He reassured himself that it was all a misunderstanding that could be sorted out with a few words. After all, what could Amelia have said to cause this utter change in Gabi?

Once Roberto drove up to the palace door, they alighted. Cesar had planned to carry his bride across the threshold, could see now that such a move would be rebuffed.

Instead he led her into the lounge.

'I'll get a fire going.'

Gabi shrugged and went and sat down, chose a single armchair, perched on the end, her hands clasped together.

'We need to talk,' he said.

'Yes,' she agreed, her voice colourless, cold, so unlike her usual tones fear gripped him again.

'I am assuming Amelia said something.' He frowned. 'What I don't understand is why you seem to have already condemned me. Without giving me a chance to explain.'

Gabi's laugh contained no mirth. 'So you can try to cast an illusory word web, spin a diplomatic codicil to our marriage agreement, a waiver, a…'

'That isn't fair.'

A shrug of her slim shoulders and then, 'OK. You're right. I suppose I should have fact-checked. Why did you split up with Lady Amelia when you did?'

The question froze him in his tracks; his brain jumping ahead, he saw the train headed down the tracks. 'It was time to end the relationship.'

'Don't play word games with me, please.' Now her voice cracked slightly, but her eyes met his, the challenge clear. 'Did you split up with her so you would be free to marry me?'

Think. But his brain refused; he knew he couldn't lie to her, knew he didn't want to. 'Yes.'

'Did you love her? Did she love you?'

'I can't answer for Amelia but I don't believe she really did love me, regardless of what she might have said. I didn't love her.' Surely she could hear the truth in his voice. But she couldn't—he could see the doubts converge in her expressive eyes, in the clench of the nails into her palms. 'Did Amelia tell you I loved her?' Dammit—he should have closed Amelia down better during the break-up conversation, had been too worried about further scandal and hadn't foreseen this.

'But you would say that, wouldn't you?' she said softly. 'You could hardly tell me, the woman you wanted to marry for political reasons, that you are in love with someone else. And you wouldn't admit it now. Because you wouldn't want to hurt me and you want to make the best of the situation.'

Somehow he had to make her see that this was not how she thought it was, but for once words wouldn't come, his brain fuzzed by panic, by the sear of guilt that he had hurt her, by the idea his marriage was already falling apart. 'I did not love Amelia.' She had to believe him. 'I had no wish to marry her. I had no wish to marry anyone.' Oh, God. That had come out wrong as well. 'Except you.'

'For duty. Because your parents told you to. For the sake of our countries.' Her voice was dull.

Try again.

'You knew this marriage was not about love, but about forging an alliance.'

She nodded. 'I did know that our marriage was based around duty but I also believed you were truly free, that your break-up with Amelia was nothing to do with me. If I had known the truth, I wouldn't have married you.'

And now he could taste the ash of bitterness in his mouth and still he couldn't find the right words to protest, to reassure, to tell her she had this all wrong. Because words had deserted him as emotions roiled.

Now he saw a tear glisten in the corner of her eye, saw her impatient swipe to get rid of it. 'I'm not sure I can be second choice. Again. For the rest of my life.'

'That's not how it is.'

'That's exactly how it is. My aunt and uncle—they were amazing people and they did do their best. But they didn't really want a child; they had their life exactly how they wanted it and they had plans. They had saved for years in order to go travelling and then retire to sunny climes. Instead they took me in, gave up their dream. For duty. To do the right thing. You are doing the same.'

Every word slammed into him as he tried to figure out the flaw in her argument, tried to work it out. 'It isn't like that.'

'To me it is exactly like that. You see…' She gave a tired smile. 'I am not trying to be difficult. But now it feels to me as though I am second best. Again. A catalyst to sending someone's life down an unwanted path. Again. I don't think I can live the rest of my life like that.'

Still no words would come. He looked at her and his heart tore. 'It wouldn't be like that.'

Another shake of her head and then she rose, the weariness evident in her movement. 'We'll talk tomorrow. I'm too tired now to find a way out of this mess. I will sleep where I slept before. Goodnight, Cesar.'

All he wanted was to move over and take her in his arms, hold her and tell her it would be all right. But he couldn't, knew it wasn't all right. Knew he had to figure out a way to make it all right, if he could just subdue the emotions that crashed and tore through him, made thought impossible, were filling him with unfamiliar panic and loss of control.

So he watched her leave, before slamming his fist into the wall.

Gabriella changed out of her going-away outfit, chosen with such care and excitement and now a garment she wished never to see again. Her movements were jerky, almost uncoordinated, as she dropped the jacket to the floor, a horrid, torrid reminder of what had started out the happiest day of her life and then degenerated into this. It would have been bad enough but what made the whole mess even worse was the fact that she loved Cesar.

Still loved him. What was she going to do? How could she spend the rest of her life with a man who loved someone else? A man who had given up his life for duty and relegated Gabi to the role of burden once again.

Her glance fell on her suitcase and the pain, the mortification intensified as she recalled the sleepwear she had brought with her. All designed for a honeymoon, for nights of decadence, for the great sex that had been on offer. Instead she pulled on jeans and a T-shirt, followed by more layers as she realised sleep would be impossible. Knew she couldn't stay here, not tonight, not on her wedding night. The urge to run was overwhelming. Necessary. She glanced out of the window. The sky looked cloudless; she knew that snow was on the way.

She and Cesar had laughed, joked about a white Christmas, about being snowed in together with nothing to do.

But the snow was not due yet and even if it came she wouldn't go far. Cesar had arranged for Ferron and Arya to be brought here so they could spend time riding on their honeymoon. She would ride just a little way, remain on royal grounds.

She added more layers, woollen ones to keep her warm, her waterproof fleece parka, woollen hat, scarf, gloves, warm riding boots, slipped out of her room and hesitated, knew that Cesar would veto this night-ride idea. But she didn't care; she had to leave. Carefully she slipped down the back stairs.

Not letting herself have time to think, she carefully

opened the front door a crack and slipped out and headed for the stables, entered and stood close by Arya, taking comfort from her uncomplicated nudge of greeting. Soon after she set off, her breath white in the dark cold air, the moonlight bright and cold on the path ahead.

Her brain hurt as she tried to see a way forward. She imagined the scandal if she ended the marriage now. Impossible. The headlines, the fallout would be too much. The only way possible would be to continue forward, trapped in a marriage she could no longer tolerate. Yet the idea of leaving Cesar wrenched her with hurt too, but better the pain now than a constant mind-numbing, soul-destroying ache of a one-sided love, in the knowledge he would have preferred a different life with a different woman but was stuck with her, putting a brave face on it. The mortification in itself stabbed her with a new pain.

The thoughts jostled and scrambled, hurled themselves round her brain. Was this how her mother had felt? All those years ago when she'd fled Casavalle, trying to decide if her marriage had been a mistake, if she could live with being a burden to the man she loved. As the thought added itself to the mix Gabi suddenly became aware of the swirl of snowflakes.

Dammit. She'd lost track of the time—come to that she'd lost track of her surroundings. A rookie mistake. Yet the snowflakes were welcome, a sudden dose of reality. What the hell was she doing? She was running away—as her mother had done. Fleeing from the problem, rather than trying to find a way to sort it out. Her mother had regretted her flight, had left it too late before she'd decided to go back. If Sophia had stayed, spoken with Vincenzo, everything could have been so different.

Gabi knew that her situation was different from her

mother's; Vincenzo and Sophia had been in love whereas Cesar didn't love her. But why was she so sure that Cesar did love Amelia? His denial had been steadfast, but it had also been clear he was racked with emotion. Her thoughts fought for clarity but could find none, yet she knew with a bone-deep certainty that Sophia would tell her to turn, go back, that running solved nothing. If Cesar did love Amelia then they still had to work out the best way forward. Together. She tugged on the reins and Arya obeyed but the snow was falling thick and fast now and Gabi felt a sudden sensation of panic. Told herself to stay calm.

It was then that the horse gave a whinny of fright. Gabi saw the glow of eyes looking at her from behind a bush and then Arya reared.

Cesar paced the spare bedroom, up and down, driven by sheer anger with himself. For messing up so spectacularly, for hurting Gabi, for not being able to make it right. Dammit, that was what he did—he made things right. And instead he'd stood there like a fool, an idiot, a gibbering, incoherent ass.

He couldn't leave it like this; he had to see her, talk to her. He pulled open his door and strode down the corridor, knocked on her door.

'Gabriella. Let me in. It's me.' He knocked again, louder this time. 'Please, Gabi. We need to talk.'

More silence. Cesar frowned. Gabriella was not the sort of woman to cower in her bedroom in silence. He tried the door, realised it wasn't locked, hesitated and pushed it open. The room was empty. The bathroom door was open and she clearly wasn't in there.

Turning, he made his way down to the lounge, the kitchen, and it was then that it struck him. She'd be in the stables. Sure he was correct, he left the castle and ran across the flagged courtyard, registered the swirl of snowfall; the cold flakes sizzled as he entered the familiar hay-scented warmth and looked round.

His heart skipped a beat as he realised Gabi wasn't there. And neither was Arya. Panic impaled him—a swirl of snowflakes could transform into a storm up here on the Aguilarean mountains and Gabriella was out there somewhere.

Fear clutched his heart, squeezed it, pulled the strings until breathing became difficult. And it was in that moment that the truth dawned on him. He loved her; he loved his wife.

Then he moved. Raced around for provisions, wrapped himself up warm and then mounted Ferron. Set off on the route he assumed she would have taken. It was impossible to see any tracks, the snow coming down too hard now, the sheer cold combated by the adrenalin that propelled him forward, calling her name. *Gabriella. Gabriella. Gabriella.* The echo seemed to get lost in the increasing deluge of snowflakes that poured relentlessly from the sky, obliterating any signs of the path Gabriella might have taken.

Bent low over Ferron's neck, he scanned the small area he could see in front of him, terrified that if she had fallen, he would miss her or, worse, trample her. Then he heard the soft thud of hooves and felt a surge of short-lived relief. It was Arya but the horse was riderless and panicked, lathered in sweat, eyes rolling, and he cursed as he managed to grab the bridle and secured her reins to Ferron's saddle. Soothed and calmed whilst inside terror raged.

Where was she? Lying somewhere injured, hurt or…

No! He would find her. Had to find her. Tell her that he loved her. Fear churned deep and cold—the idea that he wouldn't be given a chance to tell her he loved her, say the words, that he might lose Gabi, his love, his wife, his life, brought a chill sheen of moisture to his skin.

He rode on, tried to quell the rise of fear. And then out of the corner of his eye he saw something, a flicker of colour through the dense snowfall. He squinted, rode towards where he thought he'd seen it, recognised it as a scarf, a bright red woollen scarf tied around the branch of a tree. It was one of Gabi's and hope surged, along with thankfulness for her resourcefulness.

On and on they trudged, until eventually he made it to the tree, looked around, and there she was. She was scrunched in a ball; he could see that she had tried to dig out a snow cave for warmth, an action that could undoubtedly have saved her. He dismounted, tethered the horses to a tree and dropped down next to her.

'Gabriella.' His heart stopped; she lay so still, her eyes closed, her face frosted and pale and so, so cold. Worse, there was a trickle of blood on her forehead. 'Gabriella.'

Then her eyes fluttered open and she breathed his name.

'Yes, it's me. It is going to be all right. I love you, Gabi. I love you.' As he uttered the words over and over again, he lifted her up, assessed her situation quickly. Thankfully her clothing was warm, but it looked as though she'd tumbled off Arya. The forehead wound was superficial but he wasn't sure if anything else had been broken.

'Here.' He pulled out the thermos he had brought with him and held the drink to her lips. As if the smell of the hot tea woke her, she opened her eyes, looked up at him.

'Did you say you loved me?' Her smile was so sweet, so happy, she took his breath away.

'Yes, I did.'

'Good.' She sipped the tea. 'I love you too. Now I think I'll go to sleep.'

'No, Gabi. Not yet. You need to come home. With me.' She loved him. The words soared through him and he dampened the joy. *Not now.* The words could simply be born of delirium and either way his priority now was to get her home.

Somehow, by dint of coaxing and lifting, he managed to get them both up onto Ferron. Gabi, half-awake now, tried to help, but she was hampered by a twisted ankle and the fact that the cold had seeped through to her very bones.

'I love you,' he murmured again, the words so tender and so true and so blindingly obvious. He needed her to hear them, hoped she would remember them, but knew, if she didn't, he'd have the rest of his life to tell her.

But right now, as they set off on their journey back, Arya in tow, he wanted to say it all.

'I love your smile, your courage, your bravery. Love how much you care about books and literacy and your family. I love the way you frown. I love the way you have taken on your new role, your new family. I love that you have shown me that it is OK to risk my heart; I will do everything I can not to hurt you, or lose you. But if you can't love me, I'll accept that and, yes, it will hurt, but I still wouldn't change loving you. You've made me look inside myself. Made me realise that I can be more than a superficial person. It's good to make the best of things but sometimes you have to do more than that. You have to put yourself out there. And from now on I will. I want to do more for the causes I believe in. I also love your courage, the way you laugh, your inner beauty and your outer beauty, the way you lose yourself in a book. You make me happy, Gabi, and I love you with all my heart.'

Finally, they approached the castle, and he helped Gabriella off Ferron next to the stables, calling for the stable hands to take care of the horses, then gathered her into his arms, carried her across the courtyard and over the threshold. And as he did so she looked up at him and there was that beautiful smile again. 'I was hoping to be carried over the threshold,' she murmured.

Once inside he laid her gently on the sofa; soon he had a roaring fire going and then he ran upstairs and brought her down a change of clothes. On his return she was sitting up and she smiled at him, a small shy smile.

'Will you be OK if I go and make us some cocoa?'

She nodded. 'I'm feeling much better, now I've warmed up.'

'Then I'll be back in five.'

Gabi changed swiftly. The warmth had begun to permeate to her freezing limbs and extremities and her mind now buzzed. Had he meant all those beautiful words? Could he love her? Could he? What if he had just said it to get her through, keep her alert, awake. Surely not, and she allowed a tendril of joy to spread. Until another doubt raised its head. What if she'd imagined it all? Hallucinated the entire event?

She settled on the sofa, waited for Cesar to come back, stared into the leap and swirl of the red orange flames. Tried to read the future, hoped and hoped and hoped that his words had been real and true. Shyness, anticipation and hope vied with each other and her heart hop-skip-jumped and flipped as he came in.

'Is it true?' she blurted out. 'Everything you said?'

'Every word.'

'And Amelia?'

'I swear to you, Gabi, I give you my word I did not love Amelia. I have never loved any woman until you. Please believe me.'

'I do.' It was impossible not to. This man would not lie to her; sincerity blazed from his eyes and in that instant the memory of Amelia Scott-Browne was cast into oblivion.

'And… Gabi?' His unusual hesitation made her look at him closely. 'And you? Did you mean what you said? That you love me?' There was a wonder and a vulnerability in his voice that brought tears to the backs of her eyes.

'Yes. Of course I did. I love you, Cesar. I know it was not supposed to happen but it did and I couldn't have stopped it. Couldn't have stopped you from making your way into my heart.' She sipped the cocoa, savoured the warmth as he came and knelt in front of her.

'I did not know it was possible to feel this happy. This grateful that you are here. Safe. I have never been so terrified as when I thought I may have lost you. Wouldn't have the chance to tell you I love you.'

'I felt the same way. I had already decided to come back when I realised how bad the storm had become. Then Arya saw a wolf or some wild animal in the gloom and she panicked. It took me by surprise and she bolted and I came off. It took me a while to get myself together and then I realised I couldn't walk; I'd twisted my ankle too badly. I was so scared that I wouldn't be able to come back, that you'd never know I wanted to sort it out, give us a chance. It would be like my parents all over again.'

'Your parents?'

Gabi nodded. 'My mother left my father, left Casavalle because she thought it was the right thing to do. That she could never be the Queen he needed, couldn't bring her child up the royal way. But she changed her mind. She was going to come back, give it another chance. But by then my father had met Maria and she decided the best thing she could do for him was to stay away. I didn't want that to happen to us.'

'It won't.' He came and sat next to her, swung his legs up so they were side by side, snuggled under the blanket. 'It can't. Because we love each other and nothing will come in the way of that. I won't let it.' His confidence and assurance were things she loved so much about him. 'I only wish I'd realised it sooner, but, you see, I didn't think I was capable of love. The very idea terrified me—I didn't think you could feel what you haven't experienced. I couldn't see the point of risking hurt—I learnt young there was little point in getting attached to people because they leave and move on so I learnt to suppress, quell, bury any such feelings before they had a chance.'

Her heart smote her and she laid her head on his shoulder. 'I won't leave,' she promised. 'You told me all the reasons you love me. Now it's my turn. Right from that first night when I met you, you were easy to talk to. I felt comfortable around you. I trusted you. That's why I was so upset at my presentation ball, but after that you were…well, you were so much fun. I don't think I've always been very good at fun, but you've made me see how important it is. You've given me confidence, a belief that I am worthwhile, that I can do this. Can be Queen, a good ruler.'

'I know that you will be a great queen. Your sense of right, of justice, will shine through and you will make a difference to your people.'

'And you too will make a difference? Did you mean what you said earlier? About wanting to do more for the causes you believe in.' She shifted to face him. 'Because I want you to know I will support you in doing that. This marriage won't be all about you supporting me. It will be two ways. I want to help you to help others. Build a foundation, support overseas charities.'

He nodded. 'I would like to do that and I have plenty of ideas to brainstorm with you.'

'That sounds wonderful.' And it did. 'You are a caring person, Cesar. That is yet another thing I love about you. Everything you've done has been caring: the chocolates for the tree, the sleigh ride, whisking me away…'

'That's because I have loved you from the start. I have cared from the moment I saw you sprawled in the straw. I kept telling myself that I was doing all these things as part of a marriage campaign but I wasn't. I wish I had realised earlier that I loved you.' Gently he stroked her hair. 'I am so very sorry for the hurt I have caused you, for my idiocy and my clumsiness. I love you, Gabi, with all my heart.'

'It really doesn't matter—nothing matters now but this. Us. I love you so very much and I truly couldn't be happier than I am right now.' Gabi turned and brushed her lips against his, felt joy, a sense of rightness as he kissed her just as the clock chimed midnight and Christmas Day arrived.

EPILOGUE

Casavalle, January 2nd

CESAR LOOKED AROUND the table at his parents, his brothers and their families, Meribel with Dana… Flavia. His gaze travelled to take in Antonio, Tia, Luca and Imogen. Grace and Miles were also present. Meribel and Tia were deep in conversation, no doubt comparing pregnancy notes. Imogen was hand in hand with Luca. Even his parents looked more relaxed than he'd ever seen them.

The Asturiases and the Valentis…all sitting down for an informal meal following the pomp and splendour and formalities of the previous day—the day of Gabi's coronation.

And now Cesar's gaze rested on his wife and his chest swelled with pride. She had been incredible—had accepted the crown with regal grace and utter sincerity and a humble understanding of the position and duties she had sworn to uphold.

The occasion had been weighted with history. But so too was today—a meal organised by Casavalle's newly crowned Queen. No additional guests, no publicity. Just family. All eating pizza together.

Cesar wondered if his mother had ever eaten pizza

before, watching her gamely and elegantly approaching it, wielding her cutlery with grace, unfazed by the toppings falling off.

Gabi, on the other hand, picked hers up with her fingers, and to his astonishment Queen Maria followed suit.

Cesar knew that indeed times were changing.

Gabi rose to her feet and raised her glass. 'I want to thank you all; I am so incredibly happy to have you all here. My family. The Valentis and the Asturiases. United. As a small token of our appreciation Cesar and I have bought you all a gift, something small and frivolous after the ceremony and importance of yesterday.'

Cesar and Gabi had come up with the idea, wanting to introduce the concept of gift-giving to his parents, to show everyone that royalty and frivolity could go together.

Reaching under the banqueting table, Cesar picked up the bag of gifts and walked around distributing them. Amongst them was an expensive lipstick in a brighter than usual colour for his mother, an expensive set of bubble bath and shaving brushes for his dad, a beautiful friendship bracelet for Imogen, a teapot for Tia. A set of brightly coloured, vivid socks for Luca, a snow globe depicting a scene in Picco Innevato for Antonio, and a set of a slightly brighter than usual nail polishes for Maria. Every present given lots of thought.

He returned to his place next to Gabi and took out the final gift in the bag. 'For you,' he said.

'And that is for you.' She pointed to a small gift-wrapped box by his glass.

He opened it and grinned. Cufflinks in the shape of toboggans—a reminder of their first date.

Next he watched as she opened hers. A delicate charm

bracelet. The charms included a crown, a book, a horse, a plane, a toboggan, a sleigh, and of course a heart.

Gabi smiled at him, the smile that never failed to catch his breath and swell his heart with joy, and he knew he was the happiest man in the world.

* * * * *

LET'S TALK

Romance

For exclusive extracts, competitions and special offers, find us online:

f facebook.com/millsandboon

📷 @millsandboonuk

🐦 @millsandboon

Or get in touch on 0844 844 1351*

For all the latest titles coming soon, visit millsandboon.co.uk/nextmonth

Want even more
ROMANCE?

Join our bookclub today!

'Mills & Boon books, the perfect way to escape for an hour or so.'

Miss W. Dyer

'Excellent service, promptly delivered and very good subscription choices.'

Miss A. Pearson

'You get fantastic special offers and the chance to get books before they hit the shops'

Mrs V. Hall

Visit millsandbook.co.uk/Bookclub and save on brand new books.

MILLS & BOON